# The Guardians of Zenular

## Michael S. McCarty

PublishAmerica
Baltimore

© 2007 by Michael S. McCarty.
All rights reserved. No part of this book may be reproduced, stored in a retrieval system or transmitted in any form or by any means without the prior written permission of the publishers, except by a reviewer who may quote brief passages in a review to be printed in a newspaper, magazine or journal.

First printing

All characters in this book are fictitious, and any resemblance to real persons, living or dead, is coincidental.

ISBN: 1-4137-8038-5
PUBLISHED BY PUBLISHAMERICA, LLLP
www.publishamerica.com
Baltimore

Printed in the United States of America

I would like to dedicate this book to my wonderful father, who has inspired me my whole life, and give special thanks to my wonderful son, Nathaniel, who has helped me the whole way with my book.

*Michael S. McCarty*

# Contents

Story 1 ....................................................................................... 9
Chapter 1 The Twins .................................................................. 11
Chapter 2 Preparing for the Journey ........................................... 17
Chapter 3 The Journey Ahead .................................................... 21
Chapter 4 The Water Slide Out ................................................... 27
Chapter 5 Shayla's Special Gift .................................................. 30
Chapter 6 The Hidden Chamber Behind the Castle .................... 33
Chapter 7 The Enemy Gather ..................................................... 37
Story 2 ..................................................................................... 41
Chapter 1 The Fire Guardian ...................................................... 43
Chapter 2 The Serum Forest ....................................................... 47
Chapter 3 A Lost Kingdom Beneath the Fog .............................. 53
Chapter 4 Fulfilling a Destiny and Earning a New Friend .......... 57
Chapter 5 The Enemy Invades Drake's Home ............................ 61
Story 3 ..................................................................................... 69
Chapter 1 The Land Guardian .................................................... 71
Chapter 2 Another Friendship Begins ........................................ 75
Chapter 3 Meeting an Elder, Ember ........................................... 79
Chapter 4 Getting Through the Paollian Mines .......................... 83
Story 4 ..................................................................................... 91
Chapter 1 A Bounty Team for Hire ............................................ 93
Chapter 2 Here Comes a Tsunami .............................................. 96
Chapter 3 Finding a Friend in Froggle ...................................... 100
Chapter 4 Looking for the Suit ................................................. 106
Chapter 5 Finding the Element and Earning a Place ................ 110
Chapter 6 The Battle of D zan .................................................. 121
Story 5 ................................................................................... 133
Chapter 1 Whisper .................................................................... 135
Chapter 2 Finding a Key to the Past ......................................... 138
Chapter 3 The Reunion of a Lifetime ....................................... 146
Chapter 4 The Unity Is Complete ............................................. 151
Chapter 5 The Guardians Prevail .............................................. 157

# Prologue

For over a thousand years, in the farthest reaches of an unknown galaxy, lies a troubled solar system called Zenular. For it has been too long since man or beast alike have witnessed the awesome powers of the Zenular Crystals, also known as the Zenular Lights. These Crystals hold the power of the elements and life itself.

Now there is chaos and disorder throughout the solar system. Not to mention those who would do anything to get the Crystals for their own pleasure, such as the Evil Emperor, Valladamier. For with these Crystals, he could seek his revenge on his cousin, who has taken over his throne.

Now, in this time of need, the powers have awakened and soon will find the chosen beings to wield their ultimate gifts to restore peace and serenity to the Zenular solar system once again.

These are the sagas of our heroes and their friends who believe in them. This is the tale of

*The Guardians
of Zenular*

# Story 1

# Chapter 1
## The Twins

Our story starts here, on the planet of Wintox-Bora. It is the smallest of twelve planets and just so happens to be the place where our journey begins. This is where we will find Shaw and his twin sister, Shayla. They are two of the six Guardians of the Zenular Lights. Shaw and his sister will both possess the Heart Crystals, which have the power to heal all life, such as nature and beings, and with great power comes great responsibility, and very hard choices. So with this in mind, let us begin, shall we?

It was an ordinary day like any other day. The twins' mother, Lexia, and father, Toark, were out near the Setariene Caverns looking for ingredients for some potions.

"Toark, I'm going into the caverns to look for some minerals."

"All right, dear! I'll be finished here in just a few minutes. Then I shall meet up with you."

"I'll try to be quick too, dear. We really should be getting back to the children."

"You worry too much, Lexia. We put a spell over the castle right before we left, and besides, the children have Kesla and Tesla there to look after them."

"Maybe you're right. I do tend to go a little overboard, but can you

blame me? I mean, the solar system has had a lot of murderous cutthroats out there trying to find the legendary Crystals of Zenular."
"Yes, I understand, Lexia. The question is: How long till they discover that the Heart Crystal is here in Aleagra?"

Meanwhile, back at the castle, Shaw and Shayla were having some playtime with their friends, Kesla and Tesla. Now these two creatures were sisters, and they were both fairies.
Kesla was the more humble of the two. She liked to spend her time helping nature keep nurtured, while Tesla was more one with the animals. Both could talk to the plants and animals around them, and both would do anything to help out Lexia, Toark, Shaw, or Shayla...well, almost anything.

Back at the Setariene Caverns, Lexia and Toark were almost finished gathering what they needed to complete their potions.
"Lexia! Lexia honey!" Toark called out as he levitated up to the cavern entrance.
"Yes, Toark, I am over here by the Talon Crystals, getting what I need."
"All right then, dear, I shall wait for you down by Crater Lagoon."
"I'll be right there."
As Toark headed back down to the lagoon, the ground started to tremble, which did not happen all too often on Wintox-Bora anymore.
*Oh no! Lexia. I hope she is all right,* Toark thought.
"Lexia, are you all right?"
"Yes, dear! I'm okay. We should head back towards the house now, to see if the children are okay."
"You're right, let's go."
As they headed back towards their castle to check on Shaw and Shayla, a chamber opened up deep within the Setariene Caverns, and the Heart Crystal's powers came to light. The ground quake that shook the land of Aleagra, named after Lexia's great-great-grandmother, who once owned all of the land around for five miles in any direction you traveled, including Crater Lagoon and the Aleagra

Falls on the eastern side of the lagoon. This quake was caused by the Crystal as it awoke from its slumber, but not only here did this happen. The other four Crystals had also awakened. This caused quite a stir throughout the planetary system. It also caught the attention of Valladamier, who was the ruler of the star pirates in the western quadrant of the solar system. For Valladamier had been searching the solar system for the Dark Crystal of Light. It was told that there was a dark Crystal which controlled the Army of Death, and whoever should possess the Crystal would be immortal and wield great power and strength. This was exactly what Valladamier wanted, to destroy his betraying cousin Miethius, ruler of the Goyan Empire, on the Mortox Moon of the Craixe planet. This is where we will find the Fire Element Crystal later in the story. Now, we shall continue our story of Shaw and Shayla.

Back at the Aleagra Castle, Lexia and Toark had just arrived home.
"Mother, Mother, look at what Shayla did to Kesla."
"What has she done now, Shaw? Tell me."
"Follow me and I'll show you. They are in the greenhouse in the south wing."
Meanwhile, outside in the garden, Tesla had detained Toark.
"Toark, did you guys feel the ground quake?" asked Tesla, as she flew in circles around Toark with fear in her eyes.
"Yes! We felt it too! Are the children all right? Tesla, can you please stay in one spot? You are making me dizzy."
"Oh my! Please forgive me, Toark, but I am worried."
"Yes, I am too, but if what has been written is true, I am afraid the prophecy has just started."
"If you don't mind me asking, what has Lexia said about this?"
"Considering that the Heart of Light Crystal has been protected by Lexia's family for generations, and her mother being able to see into the future, well…she feels safe with it. I guess being pure of heart has its perks. As for me on the other hand, I'm more worried about Shaw and Shayla being out there on their own."
"You worry too much, Father."

"Yes, Father, it will be all right," said Shaw as he levitated down from the balcony above. "We'll be fine, Father, as you shall see. Mother has been training us for this our entire lives."

"That is right, Toark. I have taught them all they need to know about being one with the nature around them. Besides! They both have photographic memories…"

"I know, I know," said Toark as he interrupted Lexia as they walked down to the garden.

Kesla was flying right beside her. Then, out of nowhere, Toark gave out a huge laugh.

"It seems that Shayla has managed to dress you up like one of her Craixien Snap Dragons, did she? She even made you bald with a yellow and blue spotted head. How original."

"Shayla, now that you've had your fun, you can turn things back to normal again."

"Yes, Mother. Okay, Kesla, are you ready for this?"

"Oh yes, I'm ready. My head is starting to get cold."

"All right then, I'll change you back and thanks for playing with me today," Shayla replied, and with a wave of her hand, Kesla was back to her pixie self.

Kesla had long, beautiful red hair, with copper streaks in it. She also had two sets of long, silky wings, beautiful emerald-green eyes, nice pointy ears, and the softest peach skin.

"Well there. Much better now! Shall we get ready for dinner?"

As the two youngsters headed for the dining hall, Tesla and Kesla followed close behind them. Lexia took her husband by the arm and held him back.

"What is it, dear?" asked Toark.

"So who's worrying now?" asked Lexia as she passed by Toark, smiling. "It's going to be all right. They have been prepared for this moment for quite some time."

"Yes, I know, but that is not what is bothering me."

"Then what is it, my dear?"

"It's just that they haven't ever really been on their own without us being close behind. This time, there is nothing we can do if they get into any trouble."

## THE GUARDIANS OF ZENULAR

"Darling, we've got to—"

"Sorry to interrupt you two love birds, but the kids are wondering if their parents were going to join them for dinner on this fine evening."

"Oh, yes, we are, Tesla. Can you please tell them that we apologize and shall be right there? Thank you," Toark replied as he and Lexia started up the stairs towards the front door.

Suddenly, there was another slight ground quake, and a bright beam of light shot out from the caverns and straight into the watchtower, which was in the center of the castle.

"The light is shining into the watchtower. Why, no one has been up there since Grandmother passed on to the next life."

"Tesla! Get your sister and the children…"

"For goodness' sakes, Toark! They are fifteen now. We have to stop referring to them as children and remember that they are teenagers now."

"You're right again, dear, as usual," Toark answered with a smirk on his face. "Please have the young adults join us, along with you and Kesla's presence in the center watchtower."

"We'll beat you guys there," giggled Tesla as she flew away like a small streak of light, trailing across the night sky.

Within minutes, everyone was together in the tower and to everyone's disbelief, the room was lit up by the Crystal's beam of light, which struck another Crystal hanging from the top of the tower. The light shining through this Crystal illuminated a switch hidden on the wall near a portrait of Lexia's great-great-grandmother, Aleagra—Grand Mage of the Crystal Council. A secret society of very powerful wizards and mages, dedicated to keeping the Heart Crystal safe from evil and kept hidden. The light also illuminated a necklace around Aleagra's bust with two small Crystals hanging from a Chorelium chain with heart-shaped pendants around them.

Meanwhile, Shayla pressed the hidden switch and the wall moved open sideways. There was a narrow staircase leading down within the walls. It was a very short time before everyone reached a small chamber big enough to fit about forty people. Suddenly the Crystal's light faded out and with a swift pass of Lexia's wand, the torches on the wall lit up and revealed pictures and a map, leading to the path where the Crystal of Light was located. As for the Crystal's chamber, they had to find that on their own. It also gave the names of all the kingdoms protecting the armor.

It was written in the prophecy that all of the Guardians' armors were forged by ancient unknown beings, who shaped them from an unknown metal, which came directly from the largest of the solar systems two giant suns.

"Look over here, everyone."

"Wow," Shayla replied with sparkles in her eyes. "Are those what I think they are?"

"I believe so," answered Lexia as she started to reach for them. "These are the Crystals of Guidance that she wore around her neck from the portrait."

Right about that time, the stones floated up and found their way around the necks of Shaw and Shayla and at that same moment, a second door opened with a tunnel leading to an exit right inside the Setariene Caverns. This was where Shaw and Shayla were about to catch up with their destiny.

# Chapter 2
## Preparing for the Journey

The next morning, as the twins began to rise up from their sleep, a crashing noise sounded. What happened next? In came Telsa and Kelsa flying around in a big circle.

"Rise and shine you two," they were both shouting happily. "You guys have a big day ahead of you."

"Yes, and isn't it exciting to be such an important person in our future's history? I mean, everything that Shaw and I will soon be a great part of, will change the history of our home world and others in our solar system for hopefully what will be better."

"You're right. Not to mention the other Guardians, whom we've never even met yet."

"Or when we are going to meet for that matter," Shayla cut in. "Nor do we know what kind of being the other Guardians might be."

"You two have a grand adventure ahead of you," Telsa said as she landed on Shaw's shoulder. "For now though, let's not forget to clean your room and head down to the dining room hall."

As for the twins, they waved their hands and smiled as the room began to clean itself.

"I like being a mage sometimes. It has its perks."

"I agree," Shayla responded with a smile. "Shall we join everyone for breakfast now?"

"Last one there is a rotten Frawl!"

A Frawl was a little flower that grew at the base of the Aleagra Falls. As beautiful as they might look, when picked or broken by being crushed, these little beauties let off a smell that was so foul, you'd think something died. Anyhow, that gives you an idea, I hope.

Meanwhile Shaw and Shayla raced to see who was going to the dining hall first, and it was a very close race. Just as they made it to the very last turn, both of them slid and stopped. Their mouths both dropped open and their eyes wide open as they entered the room.

The two were indeed surprised. For standing in front of them were the royal families from five kingdoms on Wintox-Bora and the Emperor of the Goyan Empire on the Mortox Moon of Craixe.

"I wonder why all of these people are here."

"To see us off I guess."

"Come over here, you two," said Toark, "and take your places at the table."

As they joined their guest at the table, servants started to bring out the meals. One by one they filled the table with meats, breads, fruits, and and abundance of desserts. Everyone was eating and talking about the prophecy finally beginning and looking forward to peaceful times once again, while the twins were wondering why everyone was here to see them off. Not to mention that they would be traveling alone. When all of a sudden there was a *ting-ting* as Toark tapped his knife on the goblet.

"We are all gathered here on this beautiful morning for one reason, to see off our two future Guardians. For over a thousand years our kingdoms have stuck together in protecting each piece of the armor which the Heat Guardians will wear. Now since the prophecy has began, you all have brought with you the pieces which you have kept safe." Toark raised his hand and turned to his children and spoke out, "The time has come, my loved ones, for you both to fulfill your destinies."

Then within moments, servants came out one by one carrying boxes in their hands, from the north, the kingdom of Clauxe brought the armor pants, and from the east, the kingdom of Magel brought the shoulder and arm pieces, from the west, the kingdom of Sharex brought the chest pieces, from the south the kingdom of Arizom brought the shield and finally the last piece to each suit of armor was presented to the twins by Emperor Miethius himself.

"Well now! It seems as though something is missing here," Emperor Miethius said. "On this day your journey begins, but not without your new helmets will your armor be complete. So I hereby present you both your helmets."

Just then, as the Lord Miethius pulled the helmets from their casings, every piece of the armor began to rise up into the air above the heads of everyone in the room, and found its way onto the bodies of Shayla and her brother, Shaw. Both of the two instantly felt a power come over them, besides the fact that their armor was quite cool and very light in weight.

"This is incredible," Shaw said with excitement in his voice, "I can move around so freely. It's almost as if the armor wasn't even on my body."

"You're right. It almost feels as if the armor has become a part of us. Like it is bending with us instead of just covering our bodies."

"Yeah! I feel even stronger than I did a few minutes ago."

"Well, that's good," said Lexia to the twins. "The suits will give you both strength and invisibility. For there is nothing that can penetrate the sacred armor of Heart."

"Your mother is right. You will need the armor's protection when you two are traveling through the caverns. There are many sharp objects within the caverns."

"Not to mention many deep holes and pits one could fall into," interrupted Telsa.

"Yes! Well, let's try not to scare the kids before their journey."

"Their journey should be full of adventure, not fear. Just remember this, you two, and everything should be fine. As long as you have good faith in yourselves as well as in each other, nothing should harm either of you two."

And as he began to bow before the twins, he said this to them.

"For as long as I shall live and as long as the Goyan Empire survives, I and my Empire shall pledge our loyalty to you and the rest of the Elemental Guardians as well. For now I leave you, I must seek out three more of the Guardians as well. So if you will please excuse me, I must be going now," explained Lord Miethius as he turned away, leaving his bodyguards surrounding him.

Everyone there also had quiet a voyage home. As they all said their good-byes, they also wished the twins the best of luck, and be-carefuls, then left on their separate ways. Soon everyone was gone once again.

"Now let's get ready for you two to go on your way," Lexia told her children as she and Toark smiled and hugged their loved ones.

"Do not worry too much while we are gone."

"Yeah! We'll be fine. Besides, you both know that we are more than ready for this."

Just then, Kelsa and Telsa came flying around the corner.

"Wait! Before you leave us, we have put together some food and supplies for you," said Telsa, "Plus, we put this hologram Crystal with all of our pictures on it, just in case you start to miss us!"

"Thank you."

"Yes, thanks to all of you."

"Well then, shall we see you two off now," asked both Lexia and Toark at the same time.

"It's time to be going now."

As they headed towards the secret tunnel, everyone said their good-byes, for now.

## Chapter 3
## The Journey Ahead

As Shaw and Shayla walked along to a tunnel leading to the caverns, they began to talk.
"Shayla! Can I ask you a question?"
"You just did, Shaw," Shayla answered with a giggle.
"I'm serious, Shayla. I want to know how you feel about all of this life."
"I never really thought too much about it, brother. I never question what is to be. You of all people should know that!"
"I do know that, but that's not what I meant exactly. I mean, out of all the beings in the solar system, what makes you and me so special?"
"Just look at it like this then. Don't you feel a little better now that we were chosen, rather than the common being? I mean, our family comes from some of the most powerful mages in the system. Our Ancestors have helped to make kingdoms out there.
"We'll do just fine, brother, you shall see."
"I see some light up ahead. We are getting close to the caverns now."
"You're right. Can you feel the energy getting stronger as we get closer?"

"Yes, I can. It's almost as if the Crystal is leading us to it. When we reach the entrance to the caverns, we'll rest and snack on something before we move on. Agreed?"

"Yes, I agree. We'll rest for a short time."

As they grew closer and closer to the entrance though, it appeared that the light they saw shining in the distance was merely a crack through a rock. The entrance had buckled over time, and been sealed off.

"Wow! It seems that our exit is closed off by a cave-in."

"A little challenge for me. Stand back and watch the pro in action," said Shaw, with a silly grin on his face.

"Yeah! If you say so, my strong brother," Shayla said, laughing at Shaw.

"Okay now. Let's see what this armor can do," Shaw said as he reached out and removed the big rocks one after another. In no time, he had an opening cleared.

"There we go. Done."

"Great job, my brother," said Shayla with a smile on her face, "and you didn't even break a sweat."

"Yeah, no thanks to you."

"I'm just kidding you. Well, you did tell me to stand back. Besides, you wouldn't want me to hurt myself, would you?"

"Oh please! You can whip half of the guys, and all of the girls I know at just about everything," Shaw said proudly to Shayla.

"Thank you," said Shayla with a confused look on her face for what Shaw had just said, "for always being here for me, and for being you," Shayla said, with an even a bigger smile.

"Yuk! You're going mushy on me now," Shaw answered, giggling, "I love you too, Shayla," Shaw said as his face started to look serious. "You do know that as long as I still breathe, I will always be here for you?"

"Yes, and I for you as well," said Shayla as she handed Shaw some fruit and bread to snack on.

"What was that sound," Shaw asked as the sound grew closer to them.

"It sounded like a scouting ship," Shayla replied with concern. "Do you think whoever it is, is looking for the Crystal?"

"I'm not sure, but anything is possible, so stay alert and stay hidden," Shaw whispered to his sister as he peeked around the corner.

Then, all of a sudden, they heard two soldiers from Valladamier's army step into the caverns.

"Major Bax, sir, what exactly are we looking for here?"

"I received a big energy reading somewhere around these parts, and now it has disappeared without a trace. I just want to take a look real quick, to see if there is any more sudden energy bursts so just go back and wait by the ship for me."

"Yes, sir."

All of a sudden, there came a call over the radio from the officer by the ship.

"Major, we are being requested on Templex-Betazar for a meeting with General Ney-Glom."

"All right, soldier. Get the craft ready for flight. I'll look into this matter later. Let's go."

As they left the site and went to their spacecraft, Shaw turned to Shayla and wiped his forehead.

"That was close! It looks like we have to step it up a little. If those guys picked up the energy signature of the Heart Crystal, who knows what or who might show up next."

"I agree with you. Another thing is, how many will show?"

"Hey now! Before we get on our way, do you still have the two Crystals of guidance with you? If so, may I have one please?"

"Oh! Yes, I have them right here," answered Shayla as she handed one to Shaw. "Mother told me that in order to make them work, we must ask the Crystal to light our way."

"Okay then, ask it I will. Thank you, sis. Now let's see here. Crystal of Guidance, hear me now, and light the way to where the Heart Crystal dwells."

Just then, both of the Crystals lit up and a small beam of light came from the Crystal and lit up a dead end. As the two stopped and looked around, Shayla noticed that her helmet started to make the room more visible and so did Shaw's. It would seem that both helmets had infrared vision.

"What is happening here? This is pretty awesome."

"Mine is changing too! I can see in the dark through my helmet very well. How about you?"

"Oh yeah! This will definitely come in handy. Hey! Look over here, would you? I think I found a switch or something."

"You're right. It looks like a switch of some kind. Why don't you press it?"

Shaw then pressed down on the switch. Immediately, the wall beside Shayla began to separate. Once it was finished opening, they noticed another staircase, this time leading up. As Shaw stepped in, he shouted out, "Hello," and all of the sudden, he and Shayla heard an echoing noise and a small burst of wind. Then, a huge sum of bats came flying down at them. They both dropped to the ground as the bats kept coming and after a minute or two, the staircase tunnel was cleared.

"That was very cool," Shayla said with an amazed look about her.

"I'm glad that you enjoyed that, because I did too. Shall we continue now?"

"You lead the way and I'll follow."

"All right then, stay close to me."

As they both started up the stairs, the wall began to slide shut again. They continued to walk up around twists and turns for what felt like all day, but was really about forty-five minutes or so. Then, just as they were getting ready to ask the Crystal of Guidance for help once again, they turned the final corner and it opened up into a fairly large cavern room.

"Wait here for a moment, Shayla."

"What is wrong?"

"Nothing so far. I just want to shed some real light here. It looks like a large room or cave. Crystal, will you please light the room for me, so I can get a good look around?"

Just as he finished asking his question, the Crystal began to shine real bright.

"Oh, Shayla! Come quickly and look," Shaw said with some excitement behind his voice. "You have got to see this place."

"Oh my! It's so beautiful, Shaw. Just look at all of the different colors, sizes, and types of Crystal stones and this gorgeous lake, hidden deep inside these caverns."

"Yes, Shayla! It is very nice," Shaw said as he levitated across the lake and went on, "it looks just like a giant volcanic geode rock."

As Shaw came nearer to the shore, he noticed a warning sign of some kind.

"Shayla! Will you please join me over here?"

"Yes, brother, I'm coming," Shayla replied, and she also levitated towards her brother.

"Shayla, do you remember when we were younger and Mother taught you to read ancient writing?"

"Yes, I do, silly. You know we have photographic memories."

"That's not how I meant it. I'm serious now. Look at these markings over here on this wall. Please."

"Right away, sir...I'm sorry. I couldn't help it, seriously. Okay, be quiet now. Sorry. Now, let's see here. It says:

*He who disturbs the resting place of the Crystal of Light must be pure of heart or thou shalt perish horribly, and if pure of heart you really are, then you can stop your looking and search no more. Now turn and focus on the center of the lake as it lights up the ground and rises up from its resting place. Now, the Crystal of Light is yours to claim.*

"Shaw! Look at the ground."

"It's wonderful, isn't it?"

All of the Crystals in the cave, including in the lake, shone in every color imaginable. Then the center of the lake started to drain, creating a walkway to the box that arose from the ground in the lake. Shayla started towards the box. Shaw called out to his sister.

"Wait up for me, would you?"

"No! You hurry up and catch me."

Then Shayla turned her head back towards the box. As they got close to the box, it opened up and the champagne-colored, heart-shaped diamond separated into two halves. One half floated onto Shaw's chest armor, and the other half did the same to Shayla's chest armor. Then, suddenly, both twins were lifted up into the air, not by their own free will, but by the Crystal's power. There was light gleaming from their armor. Then they both felt this great power come over them and the light shone so bright, that it penetrated through every hole in the cave and exited through the top of the Aleagra Falls. As they began to lower back to the ground, they both knew that great things were coming their way.

## Chapter 4
## The Water Slide Out

"Hey, Shaw," shouted Shayla from the left side of the cave near a shaft that led down into an underground river.

"What's up, Shay?"

"Come over here and take a look at this, would you please? It's some sort of underground river flow from the lake."

"I see! Pretty cool."

"Aren't you the least bit curious as to where it leads? I mean, listen to the sound of its flow."

"All right, I'll listen."

As he listened to the river's rate of flow, he noticed an echo. It sounded almost as if the water was flowing down a tube.

"Yeah, I can hear what you're talking about," said Shaw with a curious look on his face. "Are you thinking what I'm thinking," asked Shaw with a look of excitement in his eyes.

"What about spikes and other sharp objects along the way? Not to mention where it will lead to."

"Well, I guess we have to trust our newfound armor and powers, and what they can do, right?"

"I'll tell you what then. Since you are the boy, I'll let you go first. If you lead, I'll be right behind you."

"Do you promise?" asked Shaw as he stepped closer and closer to the opening.

"Yes! I promise. Shaw, are you serious? Are we really going to do this?"

"Oh yeah," shouted Shaw as he turned and jumped down into the river. "Woo-hoo," screamed Shaw as he traveled down the tube. "Shayla, come on."

*Here goes nothing,* Shayla thought as she jumped into the river too. "Yeah," she shouted out with excitement in her voice, "I'm coming to get you my brother!"

"Catch me if you can, girl."

As they raced down the naturally formed waterslide, the Crystals lit the way. Within a few minutes, Shaw could see an opening, or exit you might say. It just so happened that this particular river was the mouth of the waterfall, which Shaw was soon to find out.

"Here I go," Shaw yelled out as he went over the fall. Shaw thought, *I wish I could fly right now,* when all of the sudden, he felt his body lift into the air.

"Oh yeah," he shouted out as he looped around back towards the waterfall's mouth to catch his sister as she came sailing out of the opening. Within seconds, she came out through the opening and right into her brother's arms.

"Oh my gosh! Shaw, don't drop me."

"Or what?"

"You'll find out when I…"

Just at that moment, Shaw let go of his sister and she fell fast, screaming all the way. Within a few seconds though, Shaw swooped down real fast and caught her again.

"Scared you, didn't I," he asked with a slight giggle.

"Why, if you weren't my brother, I would…"

"You would what, dear sister, turn me into something?"

"Well, I would…umm…I would…oh I don't know," she puffed, crossing her arms.

Shaw then landed safely on the ground. "That was so awesome. Let's do it again."

"No thanks! How did you do that anyway? Fly, I mean."

"I don't know really. I came through the opening and thought, *It would sure be great if I could fly right now.* Then, there I was, flying through the air. It was the most amazing thing I have ever experienced in my life so far," he replied, spinning around in circles and then falling to the ground.

He landed right on top of one of the little Frawl flowers. The air began to stink really badly. Maybe it should have been called the "foul flower." As Shayla held her nose and ran away from her brother, Shaw jumped up to his feet too, and followed her.

"Wait for me!"

"Why? You're a rotten Frawl now. Ha, ha," she laughed as she tripped over a branch lying on the ground.

"Ha, ha, ha! Who's laughing now," he asked her as he continued to laugh back at her. "See? It's true."

"What's that?"

"What goes around, comes around. You know, an eye for an eye and then some, because it comes back tenfold. Here let me help you up."

"Why thank you, sir. I appreciate the effort." Shayla smiled back as her brother gave her a lift up to her feet.

"Sure, whatever you say, sis."

"So, what now, my brother? Shall we head back home to the castle and our parents, or do we test out our new powers and abilities?"

"Let's head towards home and test everything out at the same time."

"That works for me."

They started down a narrow path back home to find out what to do next. They needed to check in the archives and find out what kind of abilities were mentioned about their powers. For you see, the abilities could change from person to person, depending on who the person was, but for now they would just have to find out on their own.

## Chapter 5
## Shayla's Special Gift

On the way back to the castle, Shayla couldn't help but wonder what it would be like when it was time for her to use her powers that were entrusted to her by some sort of higher power. Shaw was wondering the same thing.

"Shay!"

"Yes, Shaw, what is it?"

"Well...do you wonder how we will know when to use our powers or even what to do when the time comes?"

"I was just wondering the same thing myself. How strange is that? I guess when the time comes, we'll find out. I'm pretty sure everything will be as we were taught."

"I know what we were taught, but those were writings that have been passed down for over a thousand years. It's a lot different. Learning about something in a book or from scriptures is not the same as learning from mistakes, by doing it."

"I understand what you're saying, Shaw, and you're right, but I think that if we just have faith in ourselves and our abilities, the rest will fall into place when the time comes."

"When did you get so smart, my sister, who can't fly like me," he said to her as he floated up into the trees above. "So how are we going to find out what your special gift is? I have an idea."

"What is it then?"

"Maybe that's what our guidance Crystals are for. I did happen to notice a little place by the collar of our armor has a slot in it. Right here, and it looks just big enough to..." Shaw was explaining to Shayla as he took her Crystal and placed it on her armor. "There! It fits perfect. See?"

Just as he moved back away from her, Shayla began to have a vision. The Crystal started to glow. Then, just as quickly as the vision started, it ended.

"Shayla, what's going on? Are you all right?"

"I'm fine, my brother. You were right about the Crystal. Put yours in place and you shall see what I mean."

"Okay, just a moment," he said as he put the Crystal into its place.

Right at that time, his Crystal began to glow. Then, Shaw also had a vision and when he was finished, he looked at his sister and said, "Wow."

"Wow? Is that all you have to say? Just wow?"

"That was incredible, Shayla. I just saw myself using some of my abilities. What did you find out about yourself? Show me what you can do."

"Okay, give me a moment, I've never done this. Okay, here it goes."

Just then, her body began to change shape, morph you might say, into a little bird. Then she changed into a panther and after that she changed into a giant red dragon.

"Oh yeah," Shaw shouted out with excitemet.

Shayla then changed back to herself.

"Well, what do you think? Do you approve?"

"Oh yes! Heck yeah, I approve. Maybe now we can really do some good around here and anywhere else. Will you change back into a dragon and give me a lift back home, please?"

"Why? You can fly too."

"I know, but it's not like being on a dragon's back," he said to her with a gleam of hope in his eyes.

"Oh, all right. As long as you hold on tight, because it's payback time for you," she said as she snatched him up and tossed him upon her back.

For the next few minutes, Shayla flew at high speeds and high altitudes, giving her brother the ride of his life.

# Chapter 6
# The Hidden Chamber Behind the Castle

The Twins flew around for nearly an hour before they both realized that maybe it was time to get back home. As they approached the castle, Shayla soared down by the backside of the castle walls. Shaw jumped down from his sister's back. As Shayla transformed back into her usual form, she began to ask Shaw a question.

"Do you see it, Shaw?"

"Do I see what? Shayla what are you talking about?"

"The ground was illuminated around here just a moment ago," she said as she looked around. "I don't understand, I saw it."

"Maybe being a dragon had something to do with it."

"You know, maybe you're right. I mean, nobody really knows exactly what a dragon is capable of doing or seeing, right? Let me try something," she said with a slight muffle to her voice.

Shayla then began to levitate up above the ground. Then, in a calm voice, she said, "Power of Heart, give me dragon sight."

Just then a soft glow, like an aurora, surrounded her head and began to change the appearance of her eyes.

"There it is, below your feet. I can see it again, Shaw. You were right."

"Tell me then, what do you see? What is under the ground that you see?"

"It's some kind of doorway that leads underground. Move aside and I shall burn the edges around it for you. Then you can use your strength to clear the doorway," she told him as she began to change into the dragon form once again.

She then stretched her wings out, opened her mouth, and took a deep breath. Then she exhaled with some force and blew out a stream of fire, which torched the ground and lit up the sky around the castle. This got the attention of the family and the two fairy sisters, but before anyone could get to where Shaw and Shayla were, the Twins had the hidden doorway opened. It was an old marble staircase with gold hand rails running down into a twelve-by-twelve-foot chamber.

The two of them headed down the narrow spiral staircase. As they entered the room, Crystals located on the walls and on the center of the ceiling started to glow brightly. When the room was completely illuminated, our Guardians discovered yet another secret place, but this was not one that had been told about in the prophecy. It would seem that this chamber had been forgotten about. The chamber was filled with hieroglyphics and weapons. The hieroglyphics showed the Guardians how to use each weapon, and under each one of the hieroglyphics was a golden box with ancient scripture on it. As Shayla read each box, she explained it to Shaw.

Within a matter of minutes, Lexia, Toark, Tesla, and Kesla came running down the stairs.

"What is going on here," asked Toark as he came around the corner. "Shaw…and Shayla, am I glad to see you both are all right," he told them with a sigh of relief.

Right then, Lexia and the two fairy sisters entered behind him.

"It's only the kids, dear," Toark said.

"I knew that you two would be all right," said Lexia.

"Shaw! Shayla," Tesla and Kesla both yelled out at the same time, as they circled the two, rather anxious to see them. "So tell us all about your day," Tesla said.

"Yeah, tell us what happened," said Kesla.

"Was it scary?" asked Tesla.

"When you found the Crystal, was it in a beautiful golden room, with jewels and gold everywhere," asked Kesla.

Then, all of the sudden:

"Girls! Please let them rest for a moment," Lexia shouted out to them, "In the meantime, why don't you two keep a lookout for anyone above."

"Yes, ma'am," they replied as they flew up the staircase.

"Mother, will you please help me read these writings?"

"Sure I will, dear. Let me see now. What do we have here? It says here that each box contains a different weapon that can be attached to the suit of armor and easily detached for battle."

"Look here, Shaw. I've found the perfect weapons for you. I really think they will best suit your skills in battle."

"Tell me, sister, what have you chosen for me," he asked, as he started walking towards his sister.

Shayla then opened the first box, and a dim gleam of light came from within. As it opened up completely, it revealed the mythical Legendary Sword of Light.

"I thought that thing was a myth," said Toark. "This chamber is not even mentioned in the prophecy, but the weapons have been told of in stories. I always thought that they were just a myth."

"As did I," Lexia said. "I remember hearing the stories of these legendary Guardians who had weapons made by the same beings who created your armors. I have also heard that they never run out of ammo."

"What do you mean? Does it just keep reappearing or something?" asked Shaw.

"That is exactly what she means," Shayla stepped in. "According to the writings on the walls here. Look, your sword will attach itself to the backside of your armor like this."

Shayla then took the sword from her brother and placed it towards the center of her back, hilt pointing up. When she placed the sword directly behind her, it began to embed itself onto the armor, thus becoming a part of the armor. She then placed her arm behind her back again and pulled the sword back out.

"There. You see, pretty awesome, wouldn't you say?"

"Why yes, I think that is so great. Please allow me to try it now."

Shayla handed the sword back to her brother and he placed it behind his back and it joined with his suit as well.

"What else do you have for me, Shay?"

"Next, I'm giving you this crossbow along with this arrow," she told him, handing them to him. "It says that it shall be placed on your upper back, above the sword."

Shaw then placed the bow on the proper spot behind him. It also embedded itself on the armor.

"This arrow goes on your right forearm, like so," she said as she placed it onto his armor and it embedded itself onto his armor.

"It says here that every time you fire the arrow from the crossbow, it will reappear onto the armor," said Lexia, reading on. "And as for you, Shayla dear, here is a bow and four arrows. The bow is known as the Heart Bow of Streaming Light. It seems that your arrows will reappear as well, and all of your weapons have an energy-based effect when fired."

"Yes, they do," Shayla agreed. "I also have this energy-based whip, that attaches to my side."

"Why don't you to go back up and give your weapons a try? Your mother and I will conjure up some targets for you both to practice on. How does that sound?"

"That sounds all right to me," said Shaw. "What about this chamber?"

"Leave that to me, son. I shall conceal it once more. Now let's go back outside," Lexia said.

When they reached the top and sealed the entrance, Tesla and Kesla were waiting for them.

"What are you doing now, you guys?" asked Tesla.

"First, I'm going to hide the door again, and then our new Guardians are going to try out their new weapons."

"Oh no, please allow us to cover the door. Besides, we're fairies, nature is the thing we do best," Kesla said.

"Well, all right then."

They then began to fly in circles, which really was what they did best. Within moments, the grass grew itself along with flowers, covering the door completely once again.

# Chapter 7
## The Enemy Gather

On the other side of the solar system, something else was getting underway. For it seemed that Major Bax had just arrived on the moon of Templex-Betazar, at the Krokarion military base, to meet with General Ney-Glom. As his ship landed in the hangar, a small group was there to meet him.

"Major Bax, I have been sent by General Ney-Glom to escort you and your pilot to his personal quarters," said the Krokarion sergeant, as he dismissed the welcoming party.

"That will be fine," Major Bax replied. Then he turned to his pilot and said, "Stay here and watch the ship. This may be a military space station, but I still don't trust these barbarians."

"Yes, sir, Major Bax," replied the officer as he went and stood by the ship.

"Please follow me," said the sergeant.

"So, what can you tell me about these sudden energy bursts all over the system?" Major Bax asked the sergeant.

"All that I was asked to do, Major, is escort you to the general's quarters, where I was told he would be briefing you personally," the sergeant explained, as they approached the front of the general's room. "Here you go, Major. Just knock, I have to leave now. Have a good night," said the sergeant as he turned around and walked away.

As Major Bax looked towards the door, General Ney-Glom opened the door and grabbed him by the arm and pulled him inside.

"Ah! Caught you off guard, my old friend," said General Ney-Glom as he gave a short and deep laugh. "Haa! Haa! The look on your face. You almost looked as if you were getting ready to swing."

"Well, what does one expect to happen if he is caught off guard? Not to mention getting yanked by the arm into a room, which by the way, could use cleaning up. Or did you just scare the cleaning girl to death?"

"No! I didn't scare her, I ate her. Ha, ha, ha…don't worry I'm just kidding."

"So, why did you call for me to come here? Is it about all of the strange energy bursts coming and going last night and earlier today?"

"Well, if you would hold on, I will tell you. I have been up all night, trying to figure it out, and I have come to the conclusion that it is the prophecy that has begun, my friend."

"The prophecy? Don't tell me that you buy into all of the nonsense. The Crystals existing, maybe, but the Guardians? I don't believe it," with a disgusted look upon his face.

"Oh, you had better believe it to be true," came a voice from the darkness in the far right corner of the room. "The prophecy is very real, as are the Guardians," the voice said as a figure stepped out of the shadows and into the light.

The major recognized the figure standing in front of him, as he got down on one knee and said, "Valladamier…err, I mean, Emperor Valladamier. So good to see you, sir…"

"Shut up, you buffoon. Is this who you want to lead this mission for me, Ney-Glom?"

"Yes indeed. I do want Major Bax to carry out this mission. I trust no one else in the system more than I trust Bax," answered Ney-Glom, with a snarl in his voice. "I mean, not to be rude, but I trust him even more than I trust you, sir."

"Fine then," Valladamier said, and he came closer to General Ney-Glom, "He'd better not disappoint me, for your sake. If he fails, you'll die."

"Do not threaten me, Valladamier," Ney-Glom replied, as he bit down, grinding his teeth. "Have you forgotten who needs whom here? I gave you my word. If anyone can get the job done, it's Bax."

"Fine then," Valladamier said, as he nodded and then turned to Major Bax. "Major, I hope you do well. The General will fill you in on the mission's details. Good luck."

"Thanks, but I won't need luck."

Then the Emperor turned away, while two of his guards met him at the door.

"General, I do not like that guy at all. There's something not right about him."

"Ah! We're an empire of pirates and cutthroats. Since when are any of us really right?"

"Yes, but we still have codes that we live by. A certain honor amongst thieves. Besides, he used to be our enemy. Or have you forgotten the Goyan Empire he was cast out of?"

"No! That is not why we are using him. No one knows that sector of space like Valladamier does. Also, there is the most important thing of all, and that is to keep your friends and family close…"

"Yes! And keep your enemies closer. So, what is this mission that you spoke of?"

"Ah yes," said General Ney-Glom as he walked over to the window, looking out at the planet where he grew up. "Emperor Valladamier would like for you and a team of your choice to look into these sudden energy bursts. There are five different locations that he would like checked into. You have ten hours to gather your team. After that, you will report back here to me. Is that understood?"

"Yes, sir. What about all of the details?"

As General Ney-Glom headed towards the door, he answered Major Bax, "I will send the locations and planetary information to your ship's data base. Now go and be quick about it. We believe that the Crystals of Light gave off the bursts. If this is true, we must find them, before the chosen beings do. They hold powers beyond our imaginations."

"By that, do you mean the power to control the elements?"

"Yes, and who knows what else," General Ney-Glom answered with a smile and a dark gleam in his eyes. "Now go and gather the best beings you can find for the job."

"Yes, sir, General, sir," answered Bax as he got up and started out the door.

"Oh, and Bax, be careful, old friend. Just in case the Guardians have already located these Crystals."

"Okay, but why?"

"I say this because, if a Guardian has found the Crystal…" a short pause, "you and your team may not be a match up against the Zenular powers."

"We'll see, my friend, we'll see," Bax said as he turned once again and left, back to his ship.

# Story 2

# Chapter 1
## *The Fire Guardian*

On the Mortox Moon of the planet known as Craixe, was the location of the Goyan Empire. Here, Prince Lathius, son of Emperor Miethius, was getting ready to take a short trip to the Craixe planet. Here he would find our next Guardian, known as "Sergon Drake." His father, Miethius, sent him to deliver the complete suit of armor to Sergon. Unlike the armor of the Heart Guardians, which was scattered, Mietheius had the full suit of armor that belonged to the Fire Guardian, and only the helmets to the rest. Now, with that in mind, shall we begin?

It was early in the day and Prince Lathius had just left the Mortox Moon. He and a few royal guards left together in a smaller royal cruiser starship in search of Sergon Drake. Most people in his tribe just called him Drake. That was because his family came from a wealthy line of dragon herders. While Drake's family was wealthy and very well known amongst the tribe, he did not grow up as some spoiled rich kid. No, he had to work hard as a dragon trainer. He started them while they were younglings. His job was to teach them how to listen and follow commands. They would obey their masters and attack only when commanded to. Drake then taught the, I guess you could say, teenage dragons how to fly with a rider. Once they were ready, beings of all kinds traveled from all over to buy them. From the Gladius

Cluster, way over by the planet Keasar, to Kartel Nebula, just beyond the planet Cobar. Drake had earned his share of the wealth, just as his father and his grandfather did.

He had just turned twenty-three and had also heard his calling. He was almost ready to start his own destiny. In just a moment, his life would change forever. Lathius's ship approached Drake's ranch.

"Drake," one of the hired hands called out, "a royal Goyan vessel has just set down by your home."

"Thanks. I'll be right there. Come over here and watch these younglings for me until I return."

"Yes, sir."

As Drake headed towards his house, he noticed several royal guards carrying a large box. It looked rather old to him.

*I wonder what this could be about,* he thought. "Welcome, Sire. What brings you down to Craixe on this fine day? Have you come to purchase one of my top-breed dragons? Or maybe you need a flying lesson?"

Drake bowed to one knee as he stood in front of him, then got up and extended his arms and they gripped one another's arms.

"Hello, Drake. I wish I was here to buy one of your extraordinary creatures, or to have a flying lesson, but the truth is... Well, maybe we should go inside and talk."

"Very well, Sire. Please do...come in... It would seem that I have misplaced my manners today. Please forgive me," Drake said to Lathius, looking rather embarrassed.

"Oh no, Drake, it is I who must apologize to you."

"What is there for you to be sorry for and, if you don't mind me asking, what is that large box for?"

"Well, that is why I am here. Do you mind if I ask you a few simple questions?"

"Not at all, Sire. Ask me anything."

"Good, then I'll begin. Do you believe that man follows the destiny that has already been planned out for him, or do you think man creates his own destiny?"

"Well, being a man of a tribe, I believe that man follows his path chosen by the Dragon Spirit."

"That's good, because your destiny starts right now. Do you have a visible birthmark on your left shoulder which resembles a dragon? Also, do you have a Crystal shard that has been passed down to you in your possession?"

"The answers are yes and yes. Why?"

"I'm getting to that, just be patient."

"Sorry. Please continue."

"I'm pretty sure that you felt the ground quake. Am I right?"

"Yes, that's when my Crystal started glowing. Then a beam of light came out from the center of Serum Forest. The next minute it was gone."

"Let me put it to you this way. The prophecy tells of a great warrior of a native tribe, from the planet in which the fire Crystal has been hidden, he will be destined to become the Elemental Fire Guardian. He will bear the mark of the dragon upon his left shoulder and will command the dragons. A man without fear."

"Well, I must say that so far it does sound like me a little. There are plenty of guys like me. Maybe one of them bears a similar mark. What made you come to me first?"

"Well, because when the beam of light shot straight up into the sky, my station picked up the energy readings and we also picked up the same energy signature from the Crystal shard that you have as a charm. So you see, Drake, your Crystal is a part of the element. As for this crate over here... Well, let's see if you are really the chosen one. For if you are, then this is your suit of armor."

As the crate was being opened, Drake's Crystal began to glow and the armor started to rise above the ground as well as Drake. Then a gleaming light surrounded him and he floated back to the ground wearing the armor. Lathius then dropped to his knee and bowed before the Fire Guardian.

"You see, it is you. The prophecy is real and now you are one of the sacred Guardians. I will always fight by your side when you need me. I swear it on my own life. As will my father."

Drake looked into the mirror with disbelief. "I've always known deep inside me that I was destined for something great, but never this. How will I know what to do?"

"That's pretty easy to answer. The Crystal that you possess, is your Crystal of guidance. You place it on your armor, right here above your collar bone."

Right when Drake put the Crystal in place, he began to have a vision. Moments later, he snapped back from his vision.

"What happened to you, Drake? You looked out of it."

Drake then looked up at the prince and explained, "It all makes sense now, Sire. You were right. I saw what I need to do, but what about my ranch?"

"I have found some of the best dragon trainers around to look after it for you. You must go and fulfill your destiny and find the Fire Crystal before it falls into the wrong hands. I must leave now and help my father find the other three remaining Guardians," Lathius said as he bowed once more to Drake. "I wish you the best on your journey. Please make us all proud and be safe."

"I will be safe and I will bring honor to the Guardians. One more thing, I wanted to say thank you. I shall look forward to our new friendship. May it be long and good," he finished. They then grabbed each other's arms and shook good-bye.

As Lathius and his guards took the crate and left aboard his ship, Drake took a look around and walked out to the fields again. Everyone around dropped to their knees, amazed to be seeing the legendary Guardian of Fire before them. Then Drake removed his helmet and the people were even more shocked. They all got up and ran towards him, cheering for him. Drake told everyone about his destiny and that he had to leave on a trip. After he said his good-byes, Drake went out to the backside of his house and whistled.

"Manjynx, come," he shouted. "I need you, Manjynx."

Then, just over the hill to his right, came a big red dragon flying towards him, soaring through the sky.

"Good boy, Manjynx, good boy. Now listen to me, my friend, our lives are going to change now. I have a destiny to meet and I want you with me always, my good friend."

As Drake looked around one last time, he smiled, put his helmet back on, and said, "Let's fly, my friend, and meet our future," and then they flew up into the sky, where they headed to the Serum Forest.

## Chapter 2
## The Serum Forest

The Serum Forest was said to be haunted by ghosts that would take the life of anyone trying to get to Drakker Canyon, hidden somewhere in the center of the forest. You see, it was a beautiful day, but there was a fog that covered the forest as it came closer to the canyon. No one knew why, but it had always been like this. Not only that, but the winds created by the canyon made it hard for anyone to fly into it. Not to mention some of the ridge passes were too narrow for any ship to fly through without crashing due to the strong winds forcing one into the sides. To Drake and his dragon, this would be a good challenge.

    Sergon Drake had always been curious about what really went on here. Ever since he was a young boy, he heard stories of people getting lost and never returning from here. This always made him want to be the first one to make it back alive from the forest's center. As they flew on, Drake couldn't help but wonder what made him decide he was ready for this. How would he know what to do if something big happened? Yet the more he thought about it, the less it made him doubt himself. He soon came to realize that he was a strong-willed, honorable man, and if the Spirits of the Elements had chosen him out of all the other possible beings, then he would honor them as well.

    "Let's do this, Manjynx. Fly as fast as you can to Serum."

Manjynx did not even hesitate to move faster through the sky. Drake shouted out in cheer, "Woo! Woo yeah!" He held on tight and they flew for half of the day.

The first sun to go down into a sunset was the smallest of the two suns that could be seen. It was blue, still a young star. The larger sun was a soft orange color, not too long before it becames a red giant. Then when it exploded at the end of its life cycle, it would cause the younger sun to become a black hole and start to consume everything. It'd be long past when that occurred though.

As he kept on thinking, he paid attention to what was going on.

"There, my friend," he said to his dragon as he pointed to the forest.

Then the dragon spread his wings and glided down at speeds so fast that any other rider may have been blown off. Almost as if the suit was creating some type of a shield around him.

"What is this suit made of?" he asked himself, knowing that he wouldn't get an answer. At least he hoped that he wouldn't.

As they quickly approached a landing site, Drake jumped down off his dragon's back.

"Well, you must be hungry and tired, my friend. You did well, I'm proud of you. Why don't you rest here for now, and I shall catch some dinner for us. Sound good to you?"

Manjynx roared out and nodded. Then he settled down to rest. Drake walked up to his dragon and petted the side of his head.

"You have always been my best friend, Manjynx," he said to him as he hugged his dragon. "Thank you for being by my side all of these years. Now, I'm going to get us some food."

As he looked around the outskirts of Serum, he noticed a body hanging from a tree. He noticed some strange markings on the tree, but when he removed his helmet, to his surprise, the markings disappeared.

"What the heck," he said aloud. Then he put the helmet back on and the markings reappeared once again.

"Well, that's something I'll probably be thankful for later. I wonder what else I can do in this suit."

Then a soft noise came from a brush about fifty yards away.

As he tried to focus in better on the noise, his eye lens on the helmet began to zoom in on the brush.

"Now this is definitely way cool," he said under his breath.

Just then, a tri-tusk boar emerged (it got its name because not only did it have the two tusks coming from its upper jaw, but it also had a larger tusk right above its nose. This was to rip apart its prey while eating). When Drake first saw the boar, he jumped back, but only for a moment. As the beast came charging towards him, it set off a booby trap, and right as the boar hit Drake with its center tusk, and knocked him into a tree, a big spike came around the opposite side and nailed itself right into the boar's head. Drake hopped to his feet.

"I don't believe it. Ha, ha... I didn't even feel that. How do you like that? I found dinner too."

He walked over to the boar, which had to weigh around nine hundred pounds or more. Just as he got ready to call for Manjynx, he thought, *Wait a second here. If the razor end of that boar's tusk didn't hurt me, I wonder how much strength I have.*

So he went around to the other side of the giant dead boar and pushed its head off of the spike. Then he went back around again and that was when he noticed another symbol of the same origin as he had seen before. He quickly thought for just a few seconds.

"I've got it. I can't wait to tell my people what I have discovered, but first, let me give this a shot."

Then he reached down and grabbed the beast, and with no problem picked up the beast and took it back to camp. This was where he and Manjynx would stay for the night. The second sun was starting to set for the night and the first one had already passed over. He returned to the camp, with dinner in hands, and to his surprise, Manjynx had dinner ablaze for Drake already.

"So what's this? Are you implying that I'm too slow? Ha, ha... or were you just real hungry? No matter, I brought us some food for in the morning. All I have to do is find us some bird eggs and by the way, thank you for dinner, my friend. Tomorrow we shall head right through the forest and into Drakker Canyon."

As the night went on, Drake wondered what was lying ahead for him. He realized that there would be many challenges that he had to face. He also knew that he would become part of a team. A group of strangers he had never met before. Drake thought, *I wonder if the other Guardians feel like I do. Even with the power of the elements, it will take us a full lifetime, it seems, to restore order to the solar system. And will there be a chance for a family? There are so many questions going through my mind right now, but I know in my heart that everything happens for a reason and that everything will fall into place.*

All of a sudden, a scout ship passed by and from the looks of it, it was a Templexian vessel. That could only mean one thing: Ney-Glom. *But what is he sending someone here for? Could it be that he knows about the Crystal?*

"Manjynx, let's go see what's going on," Drake whispered.

On the west side of the forest, the ship set down. Four soldiers walked out of the ship.

"Sir, do you know exactly what we should be looking for?" one of the soldiers asked.

The senior officer replied, "Yes. We are looking for any strange energy reading coming from the forest. I was told to look for some type of power Crystal."

"Sir, isn't this that haunted forest people speak of?" another soldier asked.

"What do you mean haunted? Are you going to let some ghosts scare you off?"

"But, sir, they say no one ever makes it out alive, or at least no one has been found yet."

"Look, soldier, either you start walking into that forest or I'm going to kill you. Do you understand?"

"Yes, sir," the soldier said as he started heading into the forest.

Right about this time, Drake and his dragon moved in closer to hear what was going on better. As they got closer, Drake noticed a symbol upon one of the trees near the soldier coming towards him. He had to think quick or they would be discovered, so he tossed a rock over by the tree.

"What was that?" another soldier asked as he caught up with his comrade.

"I'm not sure. Let's check it out."

As they moved closer to the tree, one of them triggered a trap. Before the soldier could do anything, the ground opened up beneath them. They dropped their weapons to the side of them and fell about fifteen feet down to their deaths. They landed on top of some spikes at the bottom. This caught the attention of the other two soldiers.

"Did you hear that?" the senior officer asked.

"Yes, sir. Do you want me to check it out, sir?"

"Just wait there for a minute. I'm going to let command know that we are leaving the ship to look around."

"Yes, sir."

Within a few moments he returned. "Okay, let's go."

Back by the tree, Drake and Manjynx started backing up, when Manjynx accidentally stepped on a large fallen branch. It made a loud cracking sound. The two soldiers spotted the two of them.

"Over there!"

Then Drake turned to his dragon companion and shouted out, "Fly, Manjynx, fly," and the dragon took off into the air.

Drake ran near the hole and jumped across, grabbing one of the energy weapons that the dead soldiers dropped. It was a crossbow that shot out arrows which let off a tiny explosion on contact. Just as he was ready to shoot at the two soldiers, he noticed that Manjynx was swooping down behind them, so he backed off. The two soldiers saw Drake back off and as they both turned around, Manjynx let out a large flame from his massive mouth and torched the two soldiers to their death.

"Good work, my friend, and thank you. Soon, more ships will come. Especially when they do not report into command." He petted his dragon on the side of his head. "Well, friend, I guess it is time to move on. I think I have figured out how to get through this forest. Stay close to me and maybe you should hover off the ground just a little. This way, you won't accidentally set off any traps set around here."

Then he thought, *I'm sure grateful to the beings who left these markers here. Otherwise, I might be dead too.*

As they went through the forest, Drake was on his best alert. For it wasn't just a scout ship he had to look out for, but any more tri-tusk boars hiding in the shrubs as well. After a while, they finally came to an edge of the canyon. This is where they decided to take a short break. They looked around the canyon, a place which no one had laid eyes upon this close for centuries. Drake tried to remember what his grandfather used to tell him when he was real young. It had been about ten years since his grandfather passed away. Before he knew it, he fell asleep. Seeing him there, sleeping, Manjynx sat beside him and covered him with one of his wings. All the while watching and waiting.

# Chapter 3
# A Lost Kingdom Beneath the Fog

Several hours passed and before they knew it, the first sun started to rise. The sky almost seemed to be a violet purple, along with a dark blue, blending together in the sky, along with all of the stars shining brightly. When the light started to shine down upon Drake's face, he awoke.

"Ah, good morning, my friend. Have you been watching over me all night?"

Manjynx responded by nodding.

"Well then, I believe I owe you another thank you, so thank you. Do you want to know something, my friend? Last night, as I lay here asleep, I had a visit from my grandfather, in my dreams. He was trying to show me something. It looked like a castle in the walls of the canyon," said Drake as he paced back and forth for a moment, and all of a sudden, it dawned on him to ask his guidance Crystal, well, for help. Then, with that thought crossing his mind, he asked for help.

"Crystal of Guidance, I ask you, please show me the way."

Suddenly, the fog began to dissipate and the winds calmed around them. The fog almost spread up and over them like a cover.

"I don't believe what I am seeing, Manjynx. Shall we fly now?"

Then, without delay, Manjynx picked up Drake with his wing and tossed him upon his back and they glided down to an ancient castle carved into the canyon walls. There were giant statues on both sides. The statues all resembled the first set of Elemental Guardians.

"Could it be? Is this the sacred Lost Fortress of the Guardians?"

Most of the stories had come to pass, like most things in life. When they finally set down on the ground again, Drake looked into the sky and the fog began to cover the entire canyon again. Except, after it was all covered up, he could still see out. He was amazed at the work that must have been done to do all of this. Then he thought again, about who probably created it. Maybe the Land Guardian molded it with the power of his Crystal. Just then, his Crystal of guidance lit up and the castle doors began to open. As they entered through the doors, Drake was very cautious. For it had been many centuries since anyone had entered this fortress and from what it took to get here, he could see why.

There were a couple of torches by the doors, mounted to the walls. Drake quickly took both of them off the wall and looked at Manjynx and asked him, "Would you do the honors please," and with a silent *poof*, both torches were lit.

"Thank you, my friend. If you weren't here with me, it may have taken me all day to get those lit."

As they walked along the entryway, they glanced around the huge castle, which seemed more like a palace. There were giant pillars all over the place, carved out of the canyon bedrock itself, not placed there.

"Manjynx, can you please fly above and take a look around from an above view?"

Manjynx nodded and flew up to take a better look.

"Let me know if you see anything strange, anywhere."

There were large rooms off to the sides of the castle and in the center of the floor was a split staircase. As the staircase divided, one half went to the left and the other half went off to the right. At the end of the large room that they were in, there was another set of doors. When they reached the end, Manjynx landed by the doors, waiting for Drake to decide what they would do next. Drake just stood in front of the doors, trying to make some sense of the hieroglyphs upon their gold fronts. From what he could tell, it appeared to look like some kind of way to get the doors open. There seemed to be a place on the door for the guidance Crystal and beneath that, a place to put a right hand embedded into the wall.

Drake looked at his dragon and asked, "What do you think, my friend? Do you think the Elemental Fire Crystal is somewhere behind these doors? Or maybe just another empty room to walk through?"

Manjynx gave out a growling roar as he leaned back on his hind legs. Then he set back down and nudged at Drake to try.

"So you think I should give it a shot and see what happens next, aye?"

Manjynx roared out and nodded.

"Wow, you are pretty excited. I haven't seen you like this in some time now."

Drake then faced the doors and he took the Crystal from his suit and placed in to the slot.

"A perfect fit. Now let me place my hand on here and…"

At that instant you could see a glow around his hand and the Crystal lit up. Then there was a loud *click*, like a lock opening and then the sound of gears moving. Within just seconds, the Crystal released and fell into Drake's hand. The doors then started to open up. As the doors opened up, they began to enter. Drake held the torch up high in the air, to look for a torch upon the wall somewhere.

"Ah," he mumbled to himself. "Here we go."

Then he reached up and lit one and then went over to the other side of the door to light the next one. When the room brightened up, you could see around the room. It was more like a meeting chamber for the Guardians to take council in.

On the south wall, there were books everywhere. Like a personal library of some sort. Who knew what knowledge was written in them.

On the north wall, where the doors were, there were ancient inscriptions etched into the wall of the Guardians standing together and the solar system surrounding them. It was an awesome sight to see.

Then over on the east wall, there were small rooms that looked like small bedrooms side by side, each with a rock bed in them. Above each doorway was a symbol representing each of the Guardians.

Finally, well, almost finally, over on the west wall hung five separate tapestries. The first scenery was a picture of the Setariene Caverns along with the Aleagra Falls. The next scenery was a picture of Memtoxi-Mons, a volcano located on the planet Dazaar, which was a planet that had a lot of volcanic activity. Memtoxi was said to be the largest and tallest volcano in the solar system. It was three miles wide and eighteen miles high. The third scenery had a picture of the Paollian Mines, located on the planet Timber-Nul. The fourth scenery was a picture of the beach of Caraköl Bay, located on the Henna Moon of Kel-Tarra. The fifth scenery was a picture of the D zan Trench, located in the deepest part of the Mangalox Ocean on the planet Callegron.

Drake wondered what these pictures had to do with the Guardians. As he looked towards the center of the chamber, he saw a table. It was round and had five sections to it. Each section was designed specifically for each of the Guardians. Drake walked over to the table and looked down upon his section. He noticed a slot for his Crystal and handprint just like the door. Drake reached up and took ahold of his Crystal and placed it on the table, into the slot. Then he placed his hand over the hand scanner and the tapestry on the wall began to glow.

When Drake looked to see what was going on, he saw the volcano picture start to become a real place. As he and Manjynx stared into the picture, they both noticed a rock in the middle of a lava river and on the rock sat the Elemental Fire Crystal, a deep-red fire diamond. He realized that it was some kind of portal to collect his Crystal, but it was only big enough to fit himself through.

Then Drake turned to his loyal friend and said, "Manjynx, you stay here and watch me. I have to go alone this time, but I shall be back soon. It's time to see if this suit is what it is all cracked up to be."

Then he turned back towards the picture and jumped into it.

## Chapter 4
## Fulfilling a Destiny and Earning a New Friend

After jumping through the portal, Drake found himself on a ledge overlooking a river of lava. There were lava bubbles and flames bursting everywhere around him, not to mention the rate at which the lava flow was traveling. Drake was pretty confident that he would be able to get across to the center, where there was a large rock formation he could stand on. The only thing stopping him was his knowledge of his suit. He still wasn't quite sure how much heat or damage his suit could handle. As he waited for a plank or flat rock to drift by, he thought that he could hear something crying out. So he looked around, but he did not see anything or anyone around.

He looked back down at the lava. "Aw! There's my ride," he said to himself. Then he leaped across the lava, to a floating piece of flat rock. "Wow, come on now," he said as he tried to get his balance. "This is going to be harder than I thought. Aw," he grunted out, and he leaped towards another piece of flat rock passing by him.

Then, one last leap across to the big rock. As he jumped, his foot did not land where he had hoped and he came crashing down into the lava. Drake's heart was beating fast as he was falling, and then he hit the lava, but did not sink.

*I cannot believe it. This suit of armor is unlike anything that I have ever seen,* he thought. "I realize that I'm about to become the Fire Guardian, but honestly, I never expected this. And to top it off, the best part is that I'm not even hot. My armor still feels cool to the touch."

In his amazement, he forgot that he was standing on a river of lava. Just then, right as he was about to cross over and pick up his Crystal, he heard the same kind of cry that he heard a few moments earlier. This time, when he looked around, he saw a creature sliding down on a slope. The creature was getting close to falling over the edge.

*What to do?* he thought, as he tried to figure out a solution to help this creature.

So without delay, Drake ran across the lava towards his Elemental Crystal as fast as he could.

"I hope there's some kind of special powers that come with this," he said as he took the Crystal from its holding place.

Then, just as soon as he picked up the Crystal, he was lifted from the ground and started to illuminate. A gleaming aura surrounded him, with a blinding light covering him, until he and the Crystal became one together. When the light faded and Drake came back to the ground, he possessed all of the knowledge needed about his abilities.

"All right, now this is what I'm talking about," he said to himself as he looked back to where the creature was. "Man, I had better move quick."

Then he placed his hands down in front of his stomach and said, "Let's ride." Then a wave of lava lifted him off of his feet and he began to surf on the lava. Just as he was getting closer to the beast, it slipped and began to fall towards the lava floor. Drake had to react quickly, so he made the lava pick him up higher and whip him towards the falling creature. When he sailed closer, he grabbed hold of the creature and landed on the side of the volcano, where they made it to the rocks.

"Well now, little guy," he said to the creature as he set it down. "How did you get down here?" he asked, and right then, the little creature started to use telepathy to speak to Drake.

"Thank you, Drake!"

"How are you talking to me? You mean you can talk? But your mouth wasn't moving," he said in amazement.

"I am using our minds. I am a telepathic creature, a mystical creature one might say. My name is Dr boon. I have been placed here by the Powers that Be, 'The Creators,' which are also the ones who gave you this burden that you shall carry for the rest of your life."

"What do you mean by burden?"

"I mean spending the rest of your natural-born years dedicating your life, along with five others, to saving and cleaning up the solar system."

"Yes, but that's what it needs and I for one pledge to do my part for this team of beings I have yet to meet," he said sternly.

"Then you shall become a great Guardian, Sergon Drake, and I will serve you not only as an equal, for I have magical gifts too, but also as a companion, such as your awesome dragon Manjynx is. A pet you might say."

"So you were testing me?"

"I wanted to find out for myself if you were truly worthy of your destiny and you made good decisions on both of my tests. You showed heroism and strength, which is why you have also been chosen to take on the job as leader of this team. You show good wisdom and the Powers that Be like this."

"Then I guess I should be saying thank you."

"You are welcome, my friend, and for showing your courage, the Powers that Be would also like for your dragon to have armor as well."

In the blink of an eye, they were back in front of the table of the castle. They were standing next to Manjynx. When Dr boon bowed his head, a sparkle of light gleamed over the dragon, lifting him up off the ground. The light got real bright and then faded and Manjynx softly landed back onto the ground, transformed into the Fire Guardian Dragon. He had armor upon his head and chest. It was also on his legs. His armor matched the armor that Drake was wearing. Both were highly polished metals, with a chrome-looking finish, and red chrome flame designs on them.

"You look great in that armor, Manjynx. It makes you look even more fierce than you did before." Then he looked over at his newfound friend and pet, Dr boon. "I don't know what to say. I am at a loss for words right now."

"Well, we cannot have the Guardian of Fire going out to meet the world or the rest of the solar system without looking good, now can we?" said Dr boon, making a rhetorical statement. "Now you are ready to face the world and find the other Guardians, so that we can show them the castle of the Guardians here, where we will monitor the solar system and live from now on."

"Where shall we start?"

"We shall start at your home, where you shall find someone to carry out your responsibilities there."

"Then I say, come, Manjynx." And he hopped on top of his dragon and said, "Let's fly."

# Chapter 5
## The Enemy Invades Drake's Home

On the outskirts of Serum Forest, two scout ships were approaching at cruising speeds. They were in search of their missing team and ship.

"Sir, I've just located our missing ship," the pilot of the lead ship said.

"Then take us down slowly, Mr. Clezi."

"Yes, sir, and, sir, it looks like a battle or something went down here."

"Contact Major Bax and let him know what is going on," said Sergeant Perx, "and have the other ship fly over the forest to see if they can spot anything."

"Yes, sir."

They landed near the crash site and lowered the ship's door. Both Mr. Clezi and Sergeant Perx stepped out onto the site grounds, where they tried to figure out what happened there.

"Mr. Clezi, come take a look at these footprints," said the sergeant.

"Coming, sir."

"At ease, Clezi. It's just you and me. I want you to see these here. Take a look."

"Those prints obviously are the ones from a dragon. These footprints are from a human, but I am not to familiar with that kind of print. I mean the type of footprint, sir."

"These look like the footprints from the foot of armor. What I can't figure out though, is what would someone be in a suit of armor for."

"What do you mean, sir?"

"What I mean is, there are no beings on this planet that wear armor. Besides that, look at these two bodies and the way they were killed. They must have had their attention over this way..."

"You mean because of the blast marks on the trees over there," Mr. Clezi interrupted as he pointed into the forest about twenty-eight feet from the east of where they were standing.

"Yes! And please do not interrupt me again," Sergeant Perx said with a stern voice.

"Sorry, sir."

"Now where was I? Oh, yes. While their focus on whoever was over there, the dragon came in from behind and..."

All of a sudden, the other space craft came soaring past them overhead. It was firing its rear plasma cannons as it started to turn around. Then, from out of the tops of the trees, came our Guardian and friends. Manjynx paused in the air, with Drake still upon his back. As the ship came towards them, Manjynx filled his lungs with air and blew out a massive torch-like flame, which completely engulfed the ship, causing it to explode.

While this was going on in the sky, down below on the ground, the two soldiers were ducking for cover.

As they scuffled around, Sergeant Perx called out to his pilot, "Get back to the ship and call for reinforcements now!"

"Yes, sir."

Sergeant Perx decided it to be best if he went back to the ship also, but before he made it near the ship, he noticed something coming towards him. Running out of the forest came none other than Dr boon. As he came closer to Sergeant Perx, he jumped at him. Sergeant Perx fired his weapon, a Tulfurion crossbow, which discharged an energy blast with dual chambers. The Tulfurions were well known for their excellence in making weapons, and yet, while they created some of the best weapons in the system, they were very humble people. Every shot that Sergeant Perx fired just bounced right off of Dr boon. Then

## THE GUARDIANS OF ZENULAR

Dr boon landed right in front of him. Sergeant Perx continued to fire until Dr boon leaped at Sergeant Perx and bit him in his neck.

Meanwhile, on the ship, the pilot noticed what happened to the sergeant, then started the ship and lifted off.

As Manjynx was getting ready to inhale, Drake tapped his dragon on the neck and shouted, "Just let him go. I want him to tell everyone what he just witnessed and tell everyone the Zenular Guardians are here and are just getting warmed up."

Then they watched the ship take off real fast out of the atmosphere. Now they landed back on the ground by Dr boon.

"You did well, my friend," Drake said to Dr boon.

"Thank you. I thought you might let the ship leave."

"Yeah, well, I wanted someone to get a message across to Valladamier."

"Do you think he will get the message, that the Guardians are looking forward to taking him down?"

"It is time to stop hiding from his so-called space pirates. They are nothing more than barbarians, who have caused chaos and sorrow amongst the planetary system for two and a half decades now."

"I understand why you are frustrated, young Sergon Drake. The Powers that Be understand as well and this is why you are here now, as a Guardian. Everything happens for a reason, Drake."

"I know that," Drake said, as he looked around for any more scout ships.

"All in good time, you shall see. Just remember that we have more than just Valladamier to deal with. There are many evil, dark beings out there to worry about. Beings far worse than Valladamier. There are beings who will stop at nothing to get the Dark Crystal of Power."

"I have a question for you. Did the Powers that Be happen to tell you when or where we would meet the Guardians?"

"Yes, I have the knowledge of where and who they are, and so does Methius."

"Then maybe we should try to assemble the team, or at least find out if any of the others have obtained their Elemental Crystals yet."

"You must do this on your own, Drake. The Powers that Be

created me to help you get started on your destiny. For you are the only being that I can share words with in thought. So you see, I can help you in battle, but anything that has to do with speaking to others is your gift."

Drake had a puzzled look about his eyes. "What do you mean gift?"

"Why, the gift of speech of course. Each of your senses that you have, such as taste, smell, sight, voice, and hearing, these are all gifts given to man, and yet they take them for granted," Dr boon said as he started walking towards Manjynx.

"You're right, I never thought about it like that, I guess. Thank you, Dr boon."

"For what?"

"For helping me to realize all the poor beings out there who may need my help because they cannot all help themselves, the way I can help myself. I realize also now that I can make a difference to those who have been robbed, beaten, and pushed around by these pirates for too long. The main thing is that we get to my home and locate Prince Lathius, so we can find out where the other Guardians are," Drake explained. Then he told Dr boon to climb up on top of Manjynx and sit behind him.

"Oh yeah, Drake, there is one thing I forgot to mention."

"What is that?"

"Well, before you tell your dragon to fly as fast as he can this time, you may want to know that Manjynx's armor also gives him a special ability. He can fly at unimaginable speeds, so you had better hang on tight."

"Well, thanks for the warning," Drake answered, and he shouted, "Let's fly, Manjynx, fly on home, as fast as you can."

Then he held on to the strap attached to his saddle and they flew off real fast. Once they were up in the air at a good enough altitude, Manjynx straightened his body and extended his wings and shot through the sky at speeds of 130 per hour. As they got closer to Drake's home, it looked as if they were too late. The entire place had been destroyed. It would seem that Drake had gotten the attention of Valladamier. As they passed over Sergon's ranch, Manjynx came down to the ground and landed next to the backside of the house.

"It would seem…uhh…that someone knows who you are, Drake."

"I believe you're right. Where is everyone?"

"Drake! I sense that something has happened in the barn. You must go, now!"

"How can you tell?"

"Because I am an anima. We have strong senses for danger."

"Now hurry!"

Then Drake turned around and ran towards the barn, but when he got there, he saw blast marks on the ground caused by plasma cannons. They were made by the same kind of scout ship that they had encountered earlier that day, over by the Serum Forest. When he got to the barn doors, he pushed one of them open and witnessed a horrific sight. His workers and family (mom and dad) had all been killed. It looked like they were all hung and slit all the way down the middle. As Drake went over to where his parents were hanging, he started to tear up.

He could not help thinking, *What have I done? I never expected this to happen. I'm so sorry, Mom and Dad, for doing this to you."*

Then, as he lowered their bodies, Dr boon entered the barn.

"Drake, I'm sorry for your losses here, but just know this. You are not to blame here. There is no way that you could have changed anything that happened here. By the looks of things, all of this happened several hours ago, and whoever did this was looking for something."

"Yeah, me."

"No, they were searching for something and the young dragons you raise…"

"What about my dragons?"

"They are all missing from the nursery."

"No! They took everything I ever cared about. Yet, I will respect my parents' wishes, they told me a long time ago, and keep my head high. I know that they are in a better place now. I just wish that the rest of the Guardians and I could have already made this a better place for my parents to be. My friend, will you be so kind to please dig a few burial spots for the bodies of my family? Behind the barn is a good place. There is a hill next to it, where we can bury them.

"Yes. Is there anything else you may need as well?"

"No thank you. I'm going to look around to see if I can find out what they were looking for."

"All right then, I will do as you ask for now. When I am finished, I shall wait with your dragon until I am needed again," Dr boon said, as he left the barn and went over to the hill that Drake had mentioned.

Drake sat beside his parents' bodies for a few moments without saying anything and then stood up and walked out of the barn and headed towards the nursery. When he entered, it was empty. He picked up a few things lying on the ground. Just then, he heard a tiny chirping, crying sound, like the sound from a baby dragon. So he listened carefully for where it was coming from. As he got closer to where it was coming from, he noticed a crate turned over, by the rear windowpanes. When he lifted the crate up, he saw a baby dragon that had gotten trapped while everything was happening earlier.

"There now, little one. I am not going to hurt you. Come here now. It looks like you're the only one who made it. What should I name you? Aw, yes. I will call you Flare, because you have orange and scarlet markings upon your chest, that look like some flames. Plus, when your wings are spread like right now, it almost looks as if they have flames as well. Come on up here to my shoulder," Drake said as he set the baby dragon upon his shoulder and walked out to get his parents' bodies ready for their burial.

A little while later, Drake set their bodies into the ground and said a few words. When he was finished, Dr boon covered them up for Drake.

"Well, let me see if they found my ship as well."

Then he went over to the side of his house and opened up a little console. Then, with the push of a few buttons, a hidden door opened from the ground and up rose a small ship, just big enough to carry about three passengers and no more.

"Dr boon, will you stay here with Manjynx and look after him for me, please? I'll be back as soon as I can. I have to go up to Mortox to find Prince Lathius and discuss some things with him. I'll return as quick as I can."

"Yes, I will be right here until you return."

"Thank you. I'm going to take Flare with me," he said and he got into the ship and flew off.

# Story 3

# Chapter 1
## The Land Guardian

Our next journey brings us across the solar system to the beautiful planet of Timber-Nul. Here, we will travel to the land of Timberlan, which is located in the Shandora Mountain Range. This is where we will catch up to the Land Guardian, known as Tristan, who has already begun his journey.

Two days ago, after leaving the Twins with their armor, Emporer Methius set down on Timber-Nul to give Tristan the final piece to complete his armor. Tristan was about ninety-six years old, but he came from a race of beings that lived to become close to five hundred years of age. So, that would make Tristan about twenty-four or twenty-five in our years. He was about five and a half feet tall. He was very strong and athletic.

Tristan's home world was one of the most beautiful planets in the system. The terrain was mountainous and was mostly made up of jungles and forests. There were many different species of beings and creatures living on the planet.

There were two moons above the planet; one had life flourishing on it and the other was a dead moon. Special mining teams, wearing special gear, went to the moon to collect manicuring Crystals. These were highly radioactive stones that were transferred into raw energy that powered the starships.

So, maybe this will help you get a picture of the scenery around this story. Now back to the story.

We catch up with Tristan and his companion named "Spex." Spex was from a species of creatures that could mimic the sounds of just about everything it heard. Now try to imagine what it is like to play hide and seek with one. They were known as the Virgnomi. They usually ranged in color and looked like little gargoyles with fur. There were only about three hundred of them left in existence and they were very loyal creatures. Virgnomis only grew to be about two feet tall, but were pretty strong and lived to be about one hundred and twenty years old. Spex was already about forty-two years old and had been with Tristan for thirty-six years. They also had another gift, as you could call it. When one of them got too nervous, it would blend into its surroundings, like a chameleon. Now, where were we? Oh, yes.

Tristan and Spex had been traveling through the jungles of Timberlan for a day now. They wee approaching Mayra Canyon. From here, they would have to find the Pollian Mines. This might prove harder than it sounds. For you see, the mines were hidden somewhere in the canyon, which was covered in vegetation, steep slopes, and large serpent snakes. Some so large, that they had been known to eat a family of four cattle, plus all of the other strange creatures living there.

"Now would you look at this? Come here, my little friend, and gaze down upon this gorgeous sight. Spex, is that not a breathtaking place?"

Then Spex flapped his little wings and flew over to where Tristan was standing. As Spex looked down into the canyon, his eyes opened wide and he smiled, shaking his head up and down. Virgnomis could not talk, but they could understand very well. They were very intelligent problem solvers as well.

"It is so huge, Spex. It looks like it goes on for days. Will you fly me down to the bottom, right down there," Tristan asked, and he pointed to a small section that rounded inwards on the lower half of the cliff.

Spex then flew above Tristan's head and picked him up by the shoulders and they flew halfway down to the bottom.

## THE GUARDIANS OF ZENULAR

"Why, thank you, my friend," Tristan said as Spex released him and then landed on top of a boulder. "Are you getting hungry yet, Spex?"

Spex let out a little growl and nodded yes.

"Well, then who is going to catch dinner and who is going to set up camp for the night?"

Then, jumping up and down on the boulder, Spex decided that he would bring back dinner. Well, it was more like a late lunch and early dinner. The first sun had just passed by and the second sun was coming over them in the sky. Plus, if you looked carefully to the east, you could barely start to see the Luthor Moon coming up over the horizon.

*It will be twilight hours real soon. I need to get some rest. My body sure could use a good, hot mud bath, followed by a dip into the Quintari Hot Springs back home,* Tristan thought.

The Quintari Hot Springs were located at the base of the Mnyacari Volcano, which was about two miles from where Tristan and Spex lived. They lived in a small village called Opulence, where the men were good outdoors and the women took care of the homestead.

Tristan grew up in an adobe house built by his father. It was built right on the edge of a little cove that ran along the river basin at the bottom of the volcano. With the jungle vines hanging down over the top, it just looked like part of the volcano. No one could really see it unless they knew it was there, which also used to get Tristan's friends confused because each of the coves around it looked the same. Imagine walking outside and your friends are knocking on the rock wall in the next cove over. He would sit there and laugh at his friends, who were shouting, "Come on, Tristan. Let us in, please."

Tristan started to remember parts of his past, growing up, and one in particular made him giggle some. Around ten minutes later, Spex came back to the site where they were going to rest for the night. Spex had with him three...well, two and a half small spike-tail monkeys he had caught. Apparently he was hungrier than Tristan had thought.

"Well now, why did you not tell me that you were that hungry? We should have stopped earlier. That is all right. At least we have food right now. You did good, my friend, and thank you. Now, let me get the fire going."

Tristan pulled out a couple of stones that were in the pouch he carried around his waist. In it, he kept the two stones, which you'd strike together to get sparks, plus he always carried a few scalliums with him. He carried them in case he had to go to a trading town and get supplies. Scalliums were Crystals that had been found throughout the system and were adopted as money.

It only took but a moment for Tristan to have a fire going. He took one of the spike-tail monkeys, trying to be careful, because if one of its spike were to stick you, it would paralyze you for about two days. By then, you would probably have already become a snake's breakfast or lunch. As long as you cut off the tail, then everything would be all right. The older and bigger they got, the tougher, but the meat tasted better when it was cooked over an open flame. After dinner was finished, Tristan gathered some leaves around him and made a bed to sleep on for the night.

## Chapter 2
## Another Friendship Begins

Back on the Mortox Moon, inside the Goyan Empire, a new friendship was about to get underway. For Drake had just arrived at the landing site at the palace. As he got out of his ship, he was greeted by a rather large group of troops, along with Emperor Miethius and Prince Lathius. Everyone cheered as they met their new champion for the first time. Drake was a little embarrassed, yet he felt very comfortable inside.

"Greetings to you, Drake. I can see that you have done well in your search for the Crystal," said Emperor Miethius.

"We knew that you could do it, Drake," Prince Lathius told him. "I apologize for the way everything was handled before your journey. How did everything go?"

"Getting the Crystal was easy. It was coming home that was hard."

"What do you mean?" asked Emperor Miethius.

"Well, the night before I found the Crystal, my dragon and I had an encounter with some of Valladamier's scouts."

"What? Valladamier?" the Emperor interrupted. "What is he doing so close to here? I wonder what my evil cousin is planning. Please excuse me, I have to do something real quick."

"Yes, that is no problem, but, Sire…" Drake said with a look of sorrow in his eyes.

"What is it, Drake?"

"He had my family slaughtered and his pirates have taken all but one of my dragons."

"Oh dear," Lathius said.

"I shall send out a search team to find your dragons and your family's killers," Emperor Miethius replied. "In the meantime, why don't you go with Lathius and see what he has in store for you."

"Yes, Sire. And thank you."

"You're quite welcome, Fire Guardian." Then Emperor Miethius smiled and walked away.

Then Prince Lathius turned towards Drake and said, "Well now, Drake, you do look like a real champion in your suit of armor. How does it feel on you?"

"To tell you the truth, Sire, it does not even feel like I am wearing any armor. I really like how comfortable it is."

"Yes, well, I remember growing up as a child, looking up at the suit. I would imagine what it would be like to be a Guardian and wear the suit myself. But they were child's dreams. At least I have the honor to meet the Fire Guardian in my lifetime and hope to help you in my days left here."

"I am the one who is honored, Prince Lathius. To have a friend like you as an ally makes me feel welcome. Thank you, my friend," Drake said as they walked down the long hallway.

"Speaking of friends, there are a couple of people I would like you to meet. They are in this room over here."

"Who is it you wish for me to meet?"

"Drake, I would like you to meet your first two new partners."

As they entered the room, Shaw and Shayla were standing up and eager to meet the legendary leader, the Fire Guardian.

"Drake, I would like for you to meet the Guardians of Heart. This is Shaw and this is his twin sister, Shayla."

"Very nice to meet you," Drake said as he leaned over to Prince Lathius and whispered to him, "They are just children."

"Do not be fooled, my friend. They are both mages and very capable warriors in their knowledge of the arts. They are not to be underestimated."

"Say no more. It has been a very challenging day for me. So please forgive me if I do not seem to be so lively right now. I mourn for my parents. I just need to sit for a while."

"We understand. We shall give you time," Shaw said as he touched Drake's shoulder.

At that moment, a vision came to Drake. He saw his parents and they told him that it would be all right. As he saw them starting to fade, Drake heard his mother say, "We love you, Drake. Always keep us in your heart and there we shall always stay."

Then his father said to him, "We are proud of you, my son. Justify our deaths by doing what is right for the people and bring peace back to our world and the others around us. Trust in yourself, my dearest son, and you will achieve great things. I promise you."

Drake looked at his parents and told them, "I promise you both that I will always stay true to myself and live as a good man. I love you both," he said and then they vanished into thin air.

Shayla looked Drake and touched his arm. "Are you okay?"

"I am now," he said with a single tear in his eye and a smile upon his face. Then he picked both Shaw and Shayla up and hugged them. "Thank you."

"For what?" Shaw asked.

"I will tell you another time. In the meantime, we need to try and locate the other Guardians."

"Yes, I have someone on it already," said Prince Lathius. "We have already located one of them. Now we must wait until he locates his Crystal."

"Who is it?" Shayla asked.

"His name is Tristan. He will soon become the Land Guardian. Drake, I would like you to take Shaw and Shayla back down to your world, if you would. I would like you to show them around the Guardians' headquarters."

"Sure, I can do that. There is no point in standing here and waiting.

Besides, I still have to look around too." Then he turned towards the Twins and asked them, "Are you ready to see my home world?"

"Sure! I cannot wait to see your dragon that I have heard about," Shayla said.

"My sister can turn herself into a dragon," said Shaw.

"Wow! That sounds really cool. You will have to show me sometime. For now though, let us be on our way."

Then they all got into Drake's ship and lifted up off of the ground and flew away, back down to Craixe.

## Chapter 3
## Meeting an Elder, Ember

Back on Timber-Nul, deep inside the Timberlan Jungle, our hero was about to have himself a nice awakening. As the night turned into day, the morning light just started to break through the trees. The view overlooking the canyon was beautiful, as was the view that Tristan was about to get. As he opened his eyes, there was an ember fairy flying above his head.

"What... who...awe," he said as tried to get up.

"I'm so sorry. I did not mean to startle you, sir knight." She flew around all over the place for a moment. "What is your name? My name is Teravanna," she said as she landed on a branch not to far from where Spex was perched.

"My name is Tristan and this is my partner, Spex. You are one of the most beautiful creatures I have seen in quite some time. I take it there are more of your kind here?"

"Yes, but we live down there in the great canyon. So, what brings you here, sir knight? I do not remember seeing your face before."

"I am in search of something, little one, but I cannot say what it is. I know that does not help you very much. It is just that I cannot reveal my secret until I have completed my mission." Then he turned to Spex and said, "Spex, my friend, it is time for us to move on."

Spex stretched out his arms and little wings, then let out a big yawn. As he jumped to the ground, Teravanna flew in front of Tristan and Spex.

"Won't you both come with me to my home and have some fruit and berries to eat? You should eat before your mission."

Tristan smiled at her. "You are right, little one. We should eat before we go. It will give me some energy to get through this canyon. Thank you. You lead the way."

"Come then, follow me," said Teravanna as she started to fly down the slope."

Considering that they were already halfway down, Tristan decided he was going to ski down the rest of the way. "I will race you down, Spex," he shouted as he grabbed a couple of big leaves off of a vine and jumped on them, sliding down the slope. "I bet you cannot keep up with me, Spex."

"Graaa!" Spex cried out, then leaped into the air and began to catch up with Tristan.

Teravanna was flapping her little wings as fast as she could. Tristan was right on her dust trail, while dodging through the plants and vines, trying to keep Spex at least a full body length behind him. As they reached near the bottom, Teravanna started to slow down, but Tristan did not think about brakes. Instead, he found the generosity of a huge tree to be helpful as he so gracefully crashed into it. Spex looked at Tristan to see if he was okay and when Tristan got back onto his feet, shaking his head, Spex started laughing his tail off at what just happened.

"So you think that was funny, aye?" Spex shook his head, continuing to laugh. "I'll show you funny, mister. Get over here." Tristan started playing with Spex, trying to catch him.

"Oh my," Teravanna shouted in surprise.

"What is it?"

"How did you survive that? No regular mortal being could have lived through that crash."

Before Tristan could open his mouth to speak, an elderly woman's voice started saying, "He is not a mere mortal," she said. The eldest female and the wisest of the Embers spoke on. "For he bears the crest of the Land Guardian upon his armor. I was young when the suits were given to their chosen protectors and the Crystals were scattered and hidden throughout the system. This was also the time that the prophecy came about."

Tristan interrupted, "That would make you…around five hundred years old."

"Yes, it does make me that old."

"How is that possible? I have been told that your species only lives to be about two hundred years."

"Yes, you are again correct."

"May I know your name please?"

"My name is Delhonna Embers. I have adopted my last name by my people's request since I am the eldest." She paused for her breath.

"How is it that you know who I am?" Tristan was curious.

Spex was chasing insects around and Teravanna's eyes and attention were focused on Delhonna as she spoke. "It has been my duty, given by the Creators, to keep watch on the gate to the Emerald Land Element Crystal."

"So you know where it is that I must go?"

"Yes, and I will show you." Then she turned to Teravanna and spoke. "Teravanna, my dear."

"Yes, Delhonna? Can I get you anything?"

"No thank you, dear. What you can do for me though, is gather the others. My job here is finally done. After all of these years wondering and waiting. Now that you are finally here, I can rest now. Right over that ridge there and under the rock in the brush that is shaped like a tree." She then pointed to the east of them. "Under the vines, you will find your entrance." She coughed and took a breath.

Tristan smiled and bowed down to her. "Thank you for your kindness. I do hope you get the deserved rest you need and may your afterlife be peaceful." Then she gave him a tilt of her head to say goodbye and he was welcome.

"Wait! Do not go yet," Teravanna cried out, holding some fruits in her hands. They were wrapped in a giant leaf. "Do not forget to take some food for your mission, Sir Guardian Knight."

"Thank you, Teravanna." Then he winked at her and said, "For everything you have done."

Teravanna flew next to Delhonna, while the others kept coming as well. "You are welcome. Spex, take care of him, won't you? Make sure he does not run into any more trees, okay?" Then Spex giggled and he and Tristan started off to the cave. "Good luck," they all called out. "Good-bye!"

"Good-bye!"

# Chapter 4
## Getting Through the Paollian Mines

Just as Tristan and Spex were walking away, Delhonna called out to Tristan. "It will not be easy to find your way through the mines. The Gods have buried your Crystal well. If you wear your face shield down and look through the eye Crystal (she meant the lenses), you will see the signs they have left for you." Then she turned away and went back into the brush with her people.

Tristan told her, "Thank you again, Delhonna," as he started towards the ridge just before the entrance to the cave.

The mines were once used to get minerals from the bed rock. Then, after the mines ran dry, the first Guardians used them to get around faster, when fighting the enemy. After the wars, it became a resting place for the Elemental Land Crystal. Now Tristan had just uncovered the sealed door to the entrance.

"Well, let me see here a moment. Maybe if I put the cover down to my helmet. Awe, what do we have here? Some kind of placement for my right hand and a place for my guidance Crystal. Let me see what happens when I put this in here and my hand right here."

Then, just as he touched his hand to the stone wall, his Crystal lit up and the stone where his hand was started to glow as well. The door slid backwards. A sudden burst of wind came from the sealed cave. Then, the door began to slide to its side, along the inner wall.

"Be careful, Spex. Stay close to me," Tristan said to him as he entered the doorway. The good thing about the helmets that the Guardians had was that each was equipped with night vision. It helped even more when one already had acute vision at night, like Tristan's race of beings did. The same went for Spex's species of animal. Spex could see an ant walking along the ground in pitch black. The Vergnomi saw things based on motion at night. During the day, it was almost like they had a different set of eyes. They saw in color like most humanoid life forms did. This also made them very useful to have with you. So, as they walked completely into the mine, the door slid back into place and shut.

"We have got to find the Crystal and hope the door opens up," he said with a hint of humor in his voice. "Spex, do me a favor and fly ahead and see what is there, if you would be so kind. I am going to look for clues here." Spex nodded and flew off. "Be careful. These mines are very old."

Then he searched the walls for the hidden symbols that Delhonna spoke about. He walked for a couple of minutes, until he finally saw a mark on the wall about ten feet in front of him. Of course Spex passed right by it. He could not see the symbols as Tristan can.

"Spex," he called. "I found something over here. Spex? Do you hear me?" Spex came flying back towards where Tristan was standing. "I found a marker here on this wall. It is pointing in this direction, but it looks as though there was a cave up in there. Maybe we can get through it," he said as they started towards it. All of a sudden, Spex started getting nervous about something. "What is it, Spex?"

All of a sudden they heard a noise and then the sound of some rocks falling to the ground. "What is that, just behind the rock and beam up ahead? There is something moving over there. Do you see it too?" Tristan asked Spex as he moved closer. Spex was so nervous that he changed colors and blended in with the tunnel walls. "Where did you go, Spex?"

Right then, a twenty-seven-foot two headed Gangari python sat up, arched back and ready to strike at Tristan at any moment.

"Wow! Look at the size of you! A two-headed giant snake. What happened to you? Did you get jealous because he was better looking and beat him, or what? If it makes you feel any better, you are both ugly."

As the snake came at Tristan from both sides, he took a leap and jumped in between the two heads. As he did this though, he reached down and grabbed the snake by its tail. The snake then picked Tristan up off his feet.

"Uh oh! This is probably going to hurt."

Then the snake slammed him into the ground and picked him up again, but this time, when the snake slammed Tristan down, it caused the ground to give way. As they both fell through, Tristan grabbed a hold of the ledge on the way down. The snake still had a hold on him. The next thing you know, Spex came swooping down and bit the snake, causing it to let go. The snake fell to its death as it hit the bottom of the shaft. Tristan then pulled himself to the top of the ledge. When he was all the way to the top, he noticed that he had just found a tunnel. There was a set of marks left by the Creators. These symbols were a little different than the others. Besides that, the tunnel was more oval than square, which meant it was put there as some kind of way to get somewhere specific, without getting lost.

"Thank you, my friend. This suit is stronger than any other that I have seen before. I am just glad that I did not have to find out how strong it really is," he continued as he leaned over and gave Spex a pat on the back. "I do not know what I would do without you sometimes, old friend." Then Tristan took his guidance Crystal from his chest armor and said, "I think maybe we should shed a little light on these tunnels in these mines." He looked at Spex and smiled. "I do not need any more surprises right now. It does not matter if we have great eyesight. Someone can never tell you when extra help may come in handy." Then he held the Crystal up in front of him and said, "Guidance Crystal, will you please light the way for us? Help us stay on the right path in my quest for the Land Element Crystal."

With that said, the Crystal began to glow, but this time, about ten feet away, Tristan noticed a torch on the wall.

*How odd,* he thought as he pulled out his two stones to make a spark and hopefully ignite it. As he walked up to the torch, Spex followed close by. "Shall we give it a try?" Spex answered with a *Squawk.* "Okay then, let me give it a strike and like magic, yes, it still lights after all these centuries, undisturbed," he said aloud. Pleased that the torch lit up, he put his stones away. "Well, that is a good thing. I must say!" Spex just looked up at Tristan with a dumbfounded look upon his face, like, "Huh!"

"I am just surprised that the thing still lit after about five hundred years."

*Ooh ooh,* Spex muttered.

"Can you stay close to me this time? I am not going to have you go ahead any more. I learned my lesson. Awe, look to your left. There is another torch."

So he lit this other torch with his torch. They got about another twenty-five feet away and there was a third one. They continued to follow the tunnel all of the way until it stopped. When they reached the very end, there were two doors to choose from. This time, only one of the doors had a place to put his guidance Crystal along with his handprint.

"Well, Spex, I think this choice will be quite easy to make."

Then he placed the Crystal into its spot and put his hand on the rock door and like before, when they entered the mines, the Crystal and his handprint began to glow. Then the rock began to slide back and open. After the door had opened all the way, Tristan and Spex slowly entered the chamber. When they were all the way in, the door slid shut again. Then, Crystals that were embedded into the walls started glowing and in the center of the floor, the ground began to part. This startled Tristan for a second and then he hopped back a little. Suddenly, a panel of some kind began to rise up from the opening.

"Hey! What is going on? Something is coming up from the floor."

As the panel slowed down and locked into place, the Crystals that were on top of it started to glow. Then, a holographic map appeared, revealing where the location of the Elemental Crystal was. It also gave him the location of where he was at the moment.

"It looks like the way we need to go is through the other door, but how?" As Tristan looked down at the console, he noticed that two of the Crystals were different in size and color. He also noticed there were two spots to place these Crystals near them. "I wonder what these do." Then he took the first Crystal out, which was a light blue color, and placed it into its correct slot and the door opened behind them. "It cannot be that easy," Tristan said under his breath, and he placed the second Crystal, which was purple in color, into its spot. "No way. Spex, I do not think we were supposed to be this far yet." Spex just gave a *Squawk* and headed for the next door. "I don't know whether to thank that snake I was attacked by, or wonder what is ahead of us. Nah! Just go with the flow and see where it takes you. Although I may have a relatively long life span, I still say that life is too short to wonder all the time. Just enjoy it while you can, because the next thing that you know, it already has been and gone, my friend." Tristan grabbed the torch and followed Spex. "Am I just rambling on? Are you even listening to me? Spex...Spex, come back here." All you could hear as Spex walked away was *Squawk, squawk, squawk.* Then Spex smiled, looking forward. "I will take that as a yes." Spex just picked up the pace a little bit and kept in front of Tristan, in a subtle, teasing manor. "All right, you win. I will quit getting weird on you." Then, just to tease and play with Tristan, Spex decided to slow back down a little for Tristan to catch up. "Oh! So you do think I was rambling on, aye?" Spex then opened his eyes and squawked again, starting to jog forward. "You are just so funny, huh? I bet you just crack yourself up, right?"

Tristan began to jog after Spex and horseplayed with him. As they went on, Tristan spotted a marker on the side of another tunnel, running a different way. So they followed it down a fairly long way, until they reached the end. It was a dead end to boot. They both looked around, dumbfounded by the looks of it, but just as Spex turned around, he stepped on a switch. A trapdoor opened up and down they both fell. They fell so fast that Spex could not even catch his balance to start flying. The ride was a rather short one, but when they got to the end, they both tumbled out and ended up inside of a chamber. In this chamber, there was a picture of the Land Guardian on the west wall. Next to it was a small door, with a symbol in the center of it.

"I wonder what this symbols means." Then Spex pointed to a spot on the picture. "What is it, Spex?" He glanced at the picture closely. "I see now. Good going, Spex. It looks like the same symbol that we saw earlier." Tristan's eyes began to widen a little and so did Spex's eyes. "Are you thinking what I am?"

Then they both turned towards the door. Tristan reached out and ran his hand along the symbol. It began to glow in a green light. Then the chamber started to mildly shake for about two seconds. Then the door cracked open and a green light started shining out and Tristan started floating backwards and up to the center of the room. Spex stepped back and arched his head back some. The door opened up completely and a large green diamond floated into the air, going in circles around Tristan. A sudden blinding light surrounded him and in an instant, he came floating down to the floor again. He was now the Land Element Guardian.

"It is about time," Tristan said with a smile. "Now how do we get out of here?"

Right then, a strange light appeared from nowhere. It was a portal door and coming out of it was... "Hi there. My name is Sergon Drake and I'll be your tour guide for the evening."

"You're a Guardian?"

"Yes. Who's your little friend? It is going to be all right, my new little friend. I thought you might like to take a shortcut to our new home. This portal takes us back to the Guardians' Palace. Care to join us?"

"Us? There are more of the Guardians here as well?"

"Yes, and you will meet them real soon. Come on now. We have very little time to get everyone together and acquainted with each other. I will explain when we get to the other side." With that said, Drake jumped back trough the portal.

Tristan let Spex pass through the first and then he followed right behind. Once they were both through, the portal closed and they both hit the floor.

Drake lent Tristan a hand up. "Sorry about that," he said as he helped him to his feet. "I forgot to mention to watch your step."

Spex caught his balance and started flapping his wings. As he started to fly towards one of the chair tops, by the table, he noticed Manjynx out of the corner of his left eye, standing in the corner of the room. *Squawk! Squawk! Squawk!* Spex got himself all fluttered up.

"What is it, Spex?" Tristan asked. "What is wrong?" Then he looked over into the direction that Spex was facing. "Wow," he said, taking one step back.

"Wait," Drake said. "Please do not be afraid. He will not hurt you. This is Manjynx. He is my loyal, best friend," he said as he walked towards Manjynx, to caress his head. "He is the Dragon Guardian of Fire." Then Drake looked over towards Spex and asked, "Who is your little friend again?"

Tristan took off his helmet and said, "His name is Spex and he is my best friend."

"And you are Tristan."

This voice came from behind Tristan. Shaw came flying into the room with a hawk beside him. As they landed on the ground, Spex took a look at the hawk and felt hungry all of a sudden. So, he started creeping towards the hawk.

Right before he was ready to attack, Tristan noticed him and said, "Spex. Be polite and stay right there."

The hawk saw Spex standing there, waiting. Then the hawk began to change into a griffin. When Spex saw that happen, he went into his hiding mode and blended into his surroundings.

"By the Powers that Be. What is that?" Tristan asked.

"You mean who am I," Shayla said as she transformed back into herself. "My name is Shayla and this is my twin brother, Shaw. We are the Guardians of Heart. You must be the Guardian of Land. It is our pleasure to finally meet you."

"The pleasure is mine. You are correct, I am the Land Guardian. My name is Tristan and my friend over there is Spex. I must apologize for his manners. He means well. You just happened to look like lunch to him, that is all. So, I am curious. What are we supposed to be doing right now?"

"Well, now that we have met so far, there are still two Guardians that we still have to get. We cannot interfere until they have gotten their Crystal though. So, until then, we look around and get familiarized with this place."

"Yeah," Shaw said aloud. "I mean, that sounds good to me. Besides, you guys have to come check out some of the rooms here. They have a really cool training room."

Then Drake stepped in and said, "All in good time, young one. I think that our new friends are good and hungry by now."

"Yes, we are. Thank you." Then Spex appeared. "Oh, you finally decided to join us again."

"Yeah, and it only took the mention of food. How nice," Shayla said as she giggled.

"Then let's go find something to eat," Shaw replied.

And they all went out to catch dinner.

# Story 4

# Chapter 1
## A Bounty Team for Hire

In a remote area, located somewhere on the Taria Moon, of the planet Dazaar, lay the Valmiki Empire. Curr Valmiki was the Emperor of an empire of bounty hunters. What started as a small legion of hired bounties turned into an empire of successful bounty hunters. Some of the best men and beasts came together in council to do a job for Valladamier. Valmiki would hire out his bounty hunters to anyone, just as long as they had the right amount of scallium to pay for it. Now the team was gathered. Out of a group of thirty, Valladamier had chosen the best five to do his bidding.

"Valmiki, my old friend. It has been a long time since I have seen your face."

Valmiki extended his arm to greet Valladamier. "Yes. It has been quite some time. So, I heard that you needed help with a team of bounty hunters."

"Yes, I do. I have a very important task for your men to complete. Of course, there will be some dangers involved."

"Huh! The more danger there is, the better my men get. It is all about living and learning." He continued as he sat down in his throne, "Each time my men go into battle or on a mission, they come back stronger." Valmiki pointed to an open chair near Valladamier. "Why don't you sit down? So tell me, Lord Valladamier, what kind of task do you intend for my men?"

As Valladamier took a seat and sat back, he explained the reason for their hire. "I want your men to seek out the whereabouts of the Dark Crystal of Light for me. I also want them to first find me the Guardians and destroy them. Once I have obtained the Crystal, I will take care of my cousin, Miethius, and my nephew, Lathius, too," Valladamier said, with a look of pure hatred in his eyes.

"You're still searching for a lost dream, are you? When are you going to realize that you are chasing a dream? The prophecy is an old fable."

"Is that so? Then tell me how you explain this." He pulled out a holographic image player and slid it across the table. "Watch this and explain to me again about the prophecy being a fable."

As Valmiki picked up the device, it turned on. "What am I looking for?"

"Just wait a moment... Right there," said Valladamier as he pointed to the picture. They watched a ship flying overhead. Then, right behind them, came Manjynx and Drake. "This is footage recorded by one of General Ney-Glom's scout ships two days ago on the Craixe planet."

"I cannot believe what I am seeing here right now," said Valmiki, as he stood up from his throne. "This could bring problems to our business, if the Guardians in fact have emerged," he said as he continued to watch. They watched the dragon blow the ship out of the sky along with the help of the Fire Guardian. "Where did this Guardian come from? Has anyone seen the other Guardians? As well?"

Valladamier cleared his throat. "Uh-hum! Excuse me. Well, two days ago, a scout ship was checking on some strange energy readings. When the crew did not report in, Ney-Glom sent two more ships to investigate and this is what they found. Only one of four men sent out survived." Right at that moment, you could see Drake as the other ship got away. The ship kept recording as it flew off. "If you listen close, you can hear the Guardian say something. I had some sound work done on this footage to enhance the sounds."

As they watched on, you could hear the Guardian cry out, *"Tell Valladamier that the Guardians are coming for him."* Then it shut off. "I can see why you want my help now. If the Guardians are real, then maybe it would be a good challenge for the bounties. I will have my men meet with you at the space port. We shall talk about the fees later."

Then Valladamier extended his arm to say good-bye for now. "I shall hear from you or my men when you learn of anything," said Valmiki as he walked Valladamier to the doorway.

"In the meantime, I have some of Ney-Glom's men searching for any news about the Guardians," said Valladamier.

"Awe," Valmiki snorted. "Ney-Glom has no loyalties to anyone but himself. Just watch your back."

Then Valladamier's guards came to the door to join him. "Nice doing business with you and I will watch my back. You just worry about your men bringing me the Crystal. I hope that they do not fail either," Valladamier said, and he turned to walk away. As Valladamier closed the door and turned around, Valmiki said, "You can come out now."

Then, from a room off to the side of his chamber, a door opened and out walked Major Bax. "So, did he buy into the fact that you were going to help him?"

"Yes, he thinks that he has a chance to find the Crystal, but little does he know that it will soon be his fate that he will find. Now, take some of my men and find that Crystal before he does."

"Yes, sir. It will be my pleasure," Bax said, as he turned towards the door and left.

## Chapter 2
## Here Comes a Tsunami

We now leave our villains to join our soon to be Water Guardian on the planet called Callegron. This was a water planet, mostly, but not salt water. No, this planet was eighty-five percent fresh water and fifteen percent land. With oceans of freshwater, one would think that the polar caps would be frozen solid. Not here on this planet. With two suns in the sky and plenty of life thriving on the planet underwater, most of the water was just plain cold.

The planet was divided into three oceans with two giant landmasses dividing them from each other. The larger landmass was called Pag-wa Terria and the smaller landmass was called Tranqu-wa Terria. On the eastern side of Tranqu-wa Terria was the Mangalox Ocean. It was told that somewhere on Pag-wa Terria, there was a sea called The Sea of Tranquility. They said that if someone had any inner issues to solve, they could find their inner peace in The Sea of Tranquility. Yet, our story continues in the northern part of the Mangalox Ocean.

We travel north to the Island of Polarix. This was the burial grounds of a kingdom that once ruled all of the oceans on Callegron. No one knew what happened to this race, but they all disappeared, never to be heard from again. The kingdom was said to be cursed. Now, no one went anywhere near this island, in fear that something might happen to them. This did not stop one brave being though. This is where Emperor Miethius sent our soon to be Water Guardian with his helmet to obtain his armor. This is where we will find Tsunami.

Being part man and part water creature, he was a Pag-wa Terrian. Tsunami had light blue and beige-colored skin. He stood on two legs and walked like a man, but his body mass was triple that of a normal man. He had massive upper body strength and he was around eight and a half feet tall. His shoulders spanned about four feet wide and he could hold his breath underwater for about two and a half hours at a time. Of course he was an excellent swimmer and he could communicate with the creatures who lived underwater. So now, with this in mind, let us start the story, shall we?

As the first sun reached high noon on the planet, there seemed to be a chase taking place off the coast of Polarix. It would seem that a couple of scout ships had picked up the energy signature that came from Tsunami's guidance Crystal. They were two of Valladamier's personal army scouts. They both bore the crest that belonged to his empire. They were trailing behind Tsunami at a rather distant pace though, almost as if they expected something to happen real soon.

"VPA 65, do you see that thing anywhere," VPA 64 asked.

"Negative, sir. He must have gone under the water," VPA 65 responded.

"We will just have to wait until we reach shallower waters, which are coming up soon."

"Agreed, VPA 64. I am going to circle around to see if that thing, whatever it was, tried losing us," VPA 65 reported.

"Roger that, VPA 65 . Just be alert for anything strange going on, VPA 64 out."

The lead ship slowed its speed some. Meanwhile, the second ship fell back and began to circle around. Perhaps they were not too far off. Tsunami had gathered a couple of gigantic coral whales. This name was given to them because of their colors and markings. With one whale on each side of Tsunami, he took a hold of their fins and waited for the two ships to break off from each other. Then, as one of the ships fell back, Tsunami and the whales seized their opportunity and began to swim really fast towards the ship as it circled around. Bursting out of the water and flying up over the ship, Tsunami landed on top of the craft. The whales landed back in the water, creating a huge splash and an enormous wave. The wave crashed over the second ship, that was heading the other direction. As the water cleared from the windows of the ship, the pilot found himself heading right into the mouth of a very large sea creature. The creature then turned around and carried the ship off into the ocean depths.

Meanwhile, on the other ship, Tsunami smiled at the pilot and put his fist through the window of the cockpit. He pulled the pilot out of his seat and jumped off of the ship back towards the ocean below. As they fell towards the water, a coral whale emerged from underneath. They landed on top of the whale's back. Tsunami then held the pilot up in the air. Face to face, he snarled at him and asked, "Who sent you?"

The pilot squirmed a little, but could not get free. "Put me down!"

"I shall eat you for lunch if you do not talk now," Tsunami said in a stern voice, then opened his mouth.

"Valladamier sent us." The pilot continued to wiggle and squirm.

"What does he want with me and why could he not come himself?"

Before the pilot could speak, it looked as though he had urinated in his uniform.

"Well, now. What is this? Did you just have an accident in you pants? You weakhearted man. I'll tell you what. I will give you one chance to better your ways, so take advantage of it."

Then Tsunami tossed the pilot down on top of the whale's blow hole. The pilot reached for his weapon, pulled it out, and got to his feet. "You will pay for this, monster. You just wait and see." Then he raised his weapon towards Tsunami and got ready to fire at him.

At that moment, before he could fire it, Tsunami turned and the whale blew out a large blast of air and water. The pilot went soaring into the air and as he came down, a creature jumped out of the water, over the whale, and caught the pilot in his mouth.

"Well, you cannot say that I did not warn him," he said as he thanked his ocean friends. "I will worry about Valladamier later. Right now, I must get to the island of Polarix, where I have a date with destiny." He jumped form the whale's back and landed into the water. "Thank you, my friends, for your great help. I can make it from here. If I should need you again, you will know. Trust me." He then extended his arm, with his hand wide open, to say good-bye.

    The Coral Whales then lowered and raised their heads, making very beautiful sounds. Then they turned around and began to swim away.

## Chapter 3
## Finding a Friend in Froggle

Tsunami was very close to the shores of the island. The water started to get shallower until he reached shore. When he got out of the water, he walked over to a nearby rock and sat down. He took in a few deep breaths and rested for a short time. Next, he climbed up to the top of the hillside, where the castle gates were. Once Tsunami made it to the top, he looked for a way in.

There was a place that looked as if it may have had gates at one time. Now it was completely sealed off. The walls of the fence surrounding the castle were about fifteen feet high. Besides that, there were large spikes with hooks at the tops of them. Then, off by the corner of the wall to his right, he heard a noise coming from the brush.

So, he walked over by where it was coming from. He listened for the sound again. He heard it coming form a further spot, by the side of the castle. Tsunami picked up the pace a little and followed the sound. This time, it was more clear to him. It sounded like a cross between a cricket and a frog. As he got close to the spot where the noise came from, he saw something pass quickly through some tall grass. It was off to the right of him, in a small open field.

There were trees all around the field and one large tree, old and dead, sitting in the center of it. He jogged over to the tree, but when he got there, all he could see was a small tail with a spade-shaped fin on the end of it, going into the tree. Tsunami heard a faint splash come out of the tree. There was some moss hanging down over what looked like a hole that was created by lightning.

He pushed the moss aside to see how big the hole was. When he looked at it, he noticed that he could fit into the hole if he crouched down and crawled into it. He bent down to his knees and slid into the water. It went down like a well of some kind. *Where does it lead to and what is feeding its water supply?* he wondered. Then he sank down into the water and started to descend towards a light. As he reached the bottom of the well, the space opened up a little. As he continued to swim to the bottom, he noticed a shiny glare coming from an opening to the left side. He followed the gleam from the light. As Tsunami swam through the tunnel, he soon emerged onto a staircase leading to a couple of golden doors.

There was a crack at the top of the cave, allowing a beam of light to shine through upon the doors. As he walked up the staircase towards the doors, he caught a glimpse of a picture of the Water Guardian handing over his Crystal to the people who once thrived on the island. Then, he noticed a spot on the doors that looked as if the Crystal that he wore around his neck would fit into it. As he went to take it off his neck, he saw out of the corner of his eye the little creature standing by the side of the wall to his left. As he reached out to grab him, the creature jumped up onto Tsunami's arm.

"What are you? Can you speak?" asked Tsunami, but the creature did not answer. Tsunami had never seen a creature like this before and he couldn't communicate with him, so he was a little lost. "I will not hurt you, little guy," Tsunami said to the creature.

The creature then jumped off of Tsunami's arm and up by the doors. The little creature passed into the light so that Tsunami could get a better look at him. What he saw was a slim light green creature that looked like a frog, with hands and front arms like a gecko. His hind legs were long and muscular, yet crouched like a frog's. Plus, he had ears like a bat's and the face of a frog. His bottom feet were webbed and he had a small dorsal fin running all the way down his back. He was definitely a curious-looking creature.

"Can you speak at all?" Tsunami asked.

Then, in a mild tone, the creature asked, "Who are you? Have you come for the shiny suit that looks like your headpiece?"

It was obvious to Tsunami that this creature was a primitive being. "So you can talk. Yes, I am looking for the suit that matches my helmet. Do you know where I can find it?"

"It is beyond those doors, but you will need to open them first," the creature replied.

"How do you know it is in there and what or who are you?"

The creature then sat up on the stairs and lowered his head a little and said, "My name... I do not know my name. I do not have one. I do not even remember having one either." This caused the creature to become uneasy. He stood up and started heading for the water.

"Hey! Wait a moment. Where are you going?" Though the creature never came up from the water, Tsunami knew that he had a responsibility to perform. He also had a feeling that he had not seen the last of the creature either.

He reached out with the Crystal and placed it on the door. He waited for a moment, but nothing happened. "What is the deal with this thing?" he said aloud to himself. "Wait a minute. What do we have here? This looks like a place to put a hand, but it is way too small for my hands. Well, I guess it won't hurt to try," he said to himself as he reached out to place his hand over the other handprint's place. When he placed the Crystal back in the door, something began to happen. The place that his left hand covered began to open up to fit his hand. "Now that is more like it."

Then the doors began to open for him. As he walked through the doorway, the little creature poked its head up from the water. When Tsunami was all the way inside, the doors began to close. He looked back real quick and then kept walking. Right before the doors closed, the little creature jumped from the water and ran through the doors. He then kept a quiet pace behind Tsunami. He did not want to get caught following this giant, for he thought that he might get eaten. So for now, he was staying clear. Meanwhile, Tsunami reached into a pocket located on the right side of his vest. He pulled out two oval-shaped stones. Then he tapped them together and they began to glow brightly. "That puts some light on the subject," he said.

The room that he was standing in had statues of warriors from an ancient race of beings. Like the ones in the pictures on the doors. In the center of the room was a fire pit. He reached over to the side of the fire pit and picked up two rocks. By striking the rocks together, he made a spark. *Amazing, it actually lit up after all of these centuries,* Tsunami thought.

The flames started from the center of the pit first. Then it passed along the sides and down to the floor. Next, it traveled along the walls.

"Ouch!" a little voice came from behind a pillar. Although he was out of sight from Tsunami, he was not out of hearing range.

"Who is there? Show yourself, now," he said with a stern voice.

Then the little creature stepped out from behind the pillar with a frightened look on his face. "Please. You won't eat me, will you?"

Tsunami laughed at the creature. "If I wanted to eat you, little one, I would already have done so," he told the creature, who was standing there, shaking. "You poor thing. I did not mean to frighten you. Is that why you took off earlier? You thought that I wanted to eat you," he said as he continued to laugh. Then Tsunami took a step towards the scared creature. "It will be all right. I am just trying to see if you are okay. That is all. I promise that I will not hurt you," Tsunami tried reassuring the creature. "I give you the word of a Guardian."

"A Guardian? For what? What do you guard?"

As Tsunami started to answer the question, he thought that maybe he should reword it. "Well, let me explain to you what I am doing here first. That way, you will know better what I need to do. Earlier, you said something about a shiny suit. Do you remember?"

The creature thought for a second or two, then, "Ah! Yes, I remember now."

Tsunami nodded slightly. "Good." The creature then took a short step forward, towards what he considered to be a real giant. Though only being about fifteen inches tall, I guess everything would look rather giant to you, right? "You see, I am destined to become the Elemental Guardian of Water. I will protect our solar system with the help of some other Guardians as well," he paused, "so, you might be able to help me become this Guardian. What I want to know is, do you know where the shiny suit is at?" The creature nodded yes, his eyes wide open. "Then will you please take me to it?" Tsunami asked in a soft and pleasant manner.

The creature then pointed to a stairwell lit up by the flames. Not only did the fire light up the room, but it also looked as if it ran throughout the castle, lighting all of the borders of the floors six inches away from the wall and about another six inches wide.

"I must say that this method of lighting must be primitive to the lighting that we have now, but it is very effective. How long have you been down here?"

The creature then leaped to Tsunami's shoulder and perched himself. "If you do not mind, it is easier for me to show you from here." Tsunami put his hand up to help the creature gain balance. "I have been here for so long, that I do not know anymore. I have lost my family. We were on a ship, sailing for a new land to live on. There was a storm. It got real bad and waves were everywhere. I tried to hold on when waves came crashing on the ship. Then the ship crashed into something. I fell overboard and my family sank with the ship. I woke up here, on this land. All by myself I have been. I stay in here to keep safe from danger," the creature explained with such a sad look on his face. One could tell that he was very lonely and longed for his family.

"It must have been very frightening for all this time, being here alone."

"Oh, yes! It has."

"Well, I will be your friend. I say, it is always good to meet new beings. One can never have too many friends, you know."

The creature then lowered his head again, still with a saddened look upon his face. "No. I don't know. For I have never really had any friends."

Tsunami then lifted the creature up off of his shoulder and held him in front of his face. "I am sorry. I did not mean to make you feel bad." The creature wiped his face. "I meant that I will be your friend and soon we shall meet others too. First though, I want to do something for you." Tsunami now caught the creature's attention.

"For me, did you say? You want to do something for me? What is it," he asked again, with curious eyes.

As he looked the creature in the eyes, Tsunami said, "I would like to give you a name."

Then the creature smiled and his eyes lit up. "A name for me? Oh, that is wonderful for me," the creature said, very excited.

"First of all, I am Tsunami, and we shall call you… Hmmm, let me see here now." He thought for a moment. "I know, I shall call you Froggle. How does that sound?"

"I like it," said Froggle with an ear-to-ear grin on his face, or maybe his face always looked like that. It was hard to tell.

"Well now, my friend. Shall we go look for the suit, Froggle?"

# Chapter 4
# Looking for the Suit

After reaching the top of the stairs, Tsunami and Froggle came to a corridor. In this corridor, there were several different rooms. Tsunami looked over to his new friend and asked him, "Is any of these rooms the one we are looking for?"

Froggle shook his head no. "We must keep going. At the end, there will be a place, an open place to go. Go through it, we will, till we find the next steps to climb."

Tsunami thought that he should probably teach Froggle to speak better vocabulary sometime soon. When he had some time to do so, anyways. He continued down the corridor until he came to the end. Well, about ten feet from the end. At the end was a wall and a turned-over table with dust all over it. There was an open walkway leading to another set of stairs. This time, they spiraled up about twenty feet. Once at the top, they reached a door. This door was made from wood. Even though it was old and frail, the door still remained intact. Tsunami opened the door. Of course, Tsunami did have to crouch and turn sideways to fit through the doorway. Being so large and massive, he did that quite a bit.

"Go that way," said Froggle as he pointed towards two doors, which were across the other side of this hall of some kind.

## THE GUARDIANS OF ZENULAR

The room was bare. With nothing in there but a couple of doors, it was hard to tell what the room may have been used for. It was almost as if the former residents packed up and left the solar system and left very little, if anything, behind. The crazy thing about it though, was that there were no witnesses who saw them leave.

"This place could be a good place to live in again if it were fixed up a little," said Tsunami. As he took a few more steps, part of the floor gave way, but he got his balance back quickly. "I may have opened my mouth too soon. Now, are you sure of where we are going?"

"Yes, I am sure. I have been all over the castle since I have been here for a very long time now. I have been between walls and under the floors, but you will not fit in them. Spaces are too small for a giant like you, so I am taking you the way that fits your size."

They made it across the hall to the doors. These doors were made of wood also. "If this is the way to the room, why would it be behind wooden doors?" Tsunami said aloud to himself. When he opened the doors, there was another set of doors about five feet away. "That is more like it." In front of him was another set of golden doors. It also had one place for a hand and another for his Crystal.

"Will the door make magic lights again under your hand?"

"Let's hope so, or I will have to find a way to break these things down." Tsunami placed his hand on the door, then the Crystal.

"It is working," Froggle said.

The Crystal and the hand began to glow, then the door opened. Once inside the room, Tsunami noticed a circle on the floor. It was the symbol for the Water Guardian. A giant wave starting to break. "So tell me, friend, where did you see the suit?"

Froggle then jumped from Tsunami's shoulder to the middle of the floor. "It is under here. I saw it when I was in the walls under here."

Tsunami walked to the center of the room, where Froggle was crouched. "Then can you tell me how to get in there?"

Froggle nodded yes. Then he hopped over to a corner of the room. There was a section of the wall where a portion of the wall was covered by another. It was behind this wall that Tsunami found a panel. It had just a place for his Crystal to fit, so he placed the Crystal where it went. Next came a *BANG!*, the clicking, like gears in motion. A panel on the ceiling above was a round door that opened up. Inside was a large mirror, facing towards the sky. It was reflecting light from both suns, as they rotated around the planet. The light hit the center of the circle on the floor. When this happened, the giant symbol began to illuminate around every border of every part of the picture within it. Tsunami stayed clear of the circle, while Froggle stepped clear.

"What is happening to the ground?" Froggle asked.

Tsunami then extended his arm and said, "I do not know. Why don't you come over here and we shall find out together."

Froggle leaped over the outer portion of the circle and landed by Tsunami's feet. Then he leaped up to Tsunami's shoulder. A rather impressive jump, you might say. Then, with a look of amazement painted on both of their faces, the floor began to change right in front of their eyes.

"It is doing something," Tsunami said.

The floor started to ripple and swirl together. Everything blended together in the center of the circle and then in one motion, the floor began to crash like a wave hitting shore. When it came down, the wood turned into water. It was the most awesome sight that either of them had ever seen. Next, in the center of the pool of water, bubbles started erupting and the suit started the rise up out of the water.

"Wow! That is one bad-looking suit right there," Tsunami said. Then he started lifting off the floor. "Wait a second," he said and Froggle hopped down off Tsunami. "What is going on here? I do not do flying. Wow," Tsunami shouted as he started to spin in a slow circle with the suit in front of him.

Then he and the suit sank into the water together. A blinding light came from the water. It was so bright that Froggle could not handle it and he fell over. As the light dimmed down and the water started to settle, Froggle got back up to his hind legs. Then he could see something slowly rising from the water. It was the water Guardian, Tsunami. Froggle's eyes opened wide, for the being in front of him did not look like his friend who was just there. No! Now he looked fierce and unstoppable.

As Tsunami came up all the way out of the water, he walked across it. "What do you think, my little friend? Do you like it? I think it feels almost as if it wasn't on me."

Then Froggle stepped up to the front of Tsunami's legs and stared up at him. "It looks so shiny and it has good pictures on it."

"You mean that you like the designs on the suit of armor?"

"Yes, the pictures of waves on your body suit. It makes you look like some kind of God."

"Maybe that is because the Gods created my suit and the others like it," Tsunami said as he looked himself over in the water's reflection.

"I must say that the Powers that Be, or as you put it, the Gods, sure do have good taste," Froggle said.

"I do look quite good in it, if I do say so myself. Which I do. It feels like it is not even there. I have never owned anything like it before. Nor have I ever on Callegron seen anything else like it either. Hey, look. My guidance Crystal is here on my chest. Now where do I have to go to get my Element Crystal?"

All of the sudden, his Crystal started to glow and the pool started to ripple, just as the floor did earlier. This time though, an image appeared in the ripples. It was an image of the D zan Trench; which was not too far from where they were. It was about one half of a mile off shore from the other side of the island. Next, it displayed a map of the trench and how to get through it, to the Crystal.

"Well now, Froggle. Thank you for all of your help. See, now you have made a friend, helped make a Guardian, got a name for yourself, and found a way off of this island—all in one day," Tsunami said as he leaned over to pick him up. "That is, if you would not mind coming along with me. I would be honored if you would join me and do this with me. I am sure I will need your help again. Why, everyone needs help sometimes and others need help all of the time. So what say you, Froggle? Join me on the adventures that lie ahead?"

Then, with a tear in his eye and a smile on his face, Froggle held his head high and said, "Sure, I will go with you. We will guard everyone together with our other new friends."

## Chapter 5
## Finding the Element and
## Earning a Place

As Tsunami and Froggle make their way to the D zan Trench, we shall take a few moments and find out what our friends and foes were up to.

Back on Craixe, at the Guardians' Lair, it seemed as though everyone was getting along real well. The Twins were practicing their skills in the large area provided in the canyon around them. Covered by the fog above them, they went undetected by anyone or anything from above. They were also giving their powers some practice. The Guardians' pets also got some exercise. It would appear that Manjynx, Drãboon, and Spex were all playing a game of hide-and-seek, while Shaw and Shayla had some target practice with some tree branches and logs that Shaw flew to the top of the canyon in the Seron Forest. He made stick-men and targets for them to practice with. Meanwhile, inside the Lair, we catch up with Drake and Tristan. They had recently found a control room where they could monitor everything that went on in the planetary system. Earlier, they witnessed what went on with Tsunami and the whales. Now they had kept watch to make sure that the enemy stay clear of Tsunami achieving his destiny.

"Well, so far so good," Tristan said.

"Yeah, no more of Valladamier's scouts have come back yet," Drake replied. "It is just a matter of time before they catch on to what is going on here and start sending in armies."

Tristan then stood up from his seat, stepped to the side, and leaned against the control panel. With his arms crossed and looking at Drake, he asked him, "Do you think that the enemy will come here too?"

Drake looked him in the eyes and answered, "I am quite sure they will, but that does not bother me."

"Why is that?" Tristan asked, not knowing about the shield that covered and hid the fortress.

"Because the fortress is covered by a fog and winds that make it impossible to penetrate. Besides, if our fellow Guardian gets attacked, at least we can use the portal to get to him. If he needs help, that is."

Tristan stood up and took a deep breath. "I will be back soon. I am going to take a look outside for the first time."

Drake looked up at Tristan. "That would probably be a good idea. It will give you a chance to get some fresh air. The Twins are outside with our companions. You should try out your powers and get used to them. I am going to keep an eye on out for trouble. If anything happens, I will get you."

"I will see you soon then," Tristan said as he headed for the door.

"Have some fun too," Drake said as Tristan was leaving the room. He then looked back at the monitors to watch.

\* \* \*

Somewhere else on the other side of the solar system, in an unknown location, there was something else happening. Emperor Valladamier had called together all of the warlords to have a meeting with them. Amongst the groups of warlords was General Ney-Glom, head of the Templexian army, which was under the control of Valladamier. Then there was Chrolemius, leader of the Curon Army, and his brother, Chromwell, who led the Cobarrian Army. The two brothers were a couple of power control freaks and they both conquered their own planets. Of course, the two planets happened to be the two smallest of all of the planets. Finally, there was Valmiki, Emperor of the bounty hunters. He became a self-made Emperor by collecting the most violent and deadliest criminals in the system. He also had never been defeated in any fight or battle that he had been in. I say that would make him the most powerful ally of all.

"Now that everyone is here," said Chromwell, "what is it that you seek from us, Valladamier?"

"Yes, time is money and it is wasting away," Chrolemius added.

Valladamier then leaned over the table, placing his hands down on top of it. "If you two are finished, I will tell you," Valladamier said with a calm voice. "As you may or may not know, the prophecy is among our time. During the last week, I have met with some of you concerning certain issues. Since then, we have lost many of our scouts and ships to unfortunate events. These are events that have haunted most of our dreams for decades now."

"What are you talking about?" asked Chromwell. "I have not heard of anything strange happening around my planet," he said with a confused voice.

"I concur," added Chrollemius. "Nothing has been different on my planet either."

"Yes, well, that is why I have not mentioned anything until now," Valladamier continued. "It is my place to let you know that…" He hesitated for a moment. "Well, let me just say this. Several of the Guardians have already been seen in action."

"Wait a minute," said Chromwell. "What Guardians?"

"You idiot," Valmiki said. "Have you not been listening? He just told you that the prophecy has started. That would mean 'The Guardians of Light.' Now pay attention, you fool, and save your questions for later. That goes for you as well, Chrollemius," he said as he bowed his head for Valladamier to continue.

"Now then," Valladamier said as he brought up a map from the center of the table. "These are the locations of the sightings. All we have is the final footage from each ship, right before the were destroyed. Fortunately, none of the footage shows signs of special powers or abilities, thus far. It is only a matter of time before their powers are unleashed. When this happens, I fear what may become of us." Valladamier lowered his head, but just for a second.

"So what do you propose that we do?" asked Valmiki.

"That is a good question," Valladamier said as he looked around the table at each of them. "I propose that we join forces and send out squadrons of scouts and warriors to take them down before they gain their full powers."

"That would be wise," said General Ney-Glom. "How many have been spotted so far?"

"So far, only three have been spotted, but I fear the rest are going to appear soon too. That is why we must work together quickly and save ourselves the trouble of losing any more men than needed." Valladamier then placed his fist upon the table. "Agreed?"

"Yes," they all said one by one.

"Then let's get it started as soon as possible.

They all got up from their seats and said their final words, before leaving back to their homes.

\* \* \*

Back on Callegron, we catch up to Tsunami and Froggle again. This time, they reached the entrance to the D zan Trench. The trench was darkened by the shadows of its own walls. There were many different creatures who lived within this trench. The good thing about it though, was that Tsunami was born with the gift to understand and communicate with most of the creatures that dwelled here. Although, there were some that he could not talk to. Most of them lived deeper in the trench. This was a good thing as well. As for any enemy coming for him, they would not have such good luck. Tsunami and Froggle got ready to go inside. "If you stay by my side, then you will be safe," Tsunami said to Froggle, who seemed scared.

"All right then. I will stay real close to you. As a matter of fact, me was wondering if I can ride on your back?"

Tsunami told Froggle to wait there for a minute, then he swam to the top of the trench and picked a couple of vines from one of the plants. He swam back to where Froggle was. "Here, wrap these around yourself and then give the end straps to me. I will need to tie you to me so I can swim faster. So you had better hold on to me."

Froggle then grabbed on to him and Tsunami took off real fast. He traveled right into the center of the trench. The D zan Trench was too dangerous for most to enter. Besides the many creatures that lived there, it also possessed a few different underwater caves within it. Three of them were on the east side of the trench, while the fourth one was located on the west side of the trench. This one was filled with water and one of the other three was also filled with water. However, neither Tsunami nor Froggle had any idea which one it was. Now they would have to find out because the map that Tsunami had only showed him where the Crystal was, not which entrance to take.

"Well now, how are you doing? I can see that you held on tight. I was not sure if you were still with me or not," Tsunami said as he loosened the vines and freed Froggle from him.

"I must say, you give a good ride. Maybe you should sell rides instead," Froggle said with a big grin on his face.

Tsunami then touched his hand to his chest and asked his guidance Crystal to show him the way to his Crystal. "What?" he said with a look of surprise on his face. "The light shines through two of the cave entrances. How can this be? Why would the Crystal shine in two separate caves?"

"Maybe they are one cave with two entrances."

"That could be possible too. Just remember to stay close and keep your eyes open for me," Tsunami told Froggle as he entered the first cave, which was to the north of them. "Okay?"

"Okay."

Although the helmet provided night vision, Tsunami preferred to have natural light. Once again, he pulled out the two stones from earlier. He rubbed the stones together and they started to glow. When the light came on, several small schools of fish began to scatter. In this cave, there were several small tunnels leading off in different directions.

Being undecided on which one to take, Tsunami sought the

guidance of his Crystal once again. "Guidance Crystal, will you show me which tunnel to take?" Then the Crystal sent out a narrow beam. It shone on the tunnel that was in front of them.

"It looks like we take that entrance up there," said Froggle.

"That is right. Would you like to go first?" Tsunami asked jokingly. The look on Froggle's face made Tsunami laugh. "Do not worry yourself, my friend. I was playing with you."

"You were only joking?"

"Yes, I was, but you can do me one thing, though," said Tsunami as he reached his arm out to hand Froggle his stones, which produced light. "If I place you upon my shoulders, then you could hold the light up higher. This way, it gives off more light and it frees up my hands.."

"All right, I can do it. Besides, this way, I do not get lost."

Good thing that there were natural air-filled pockets within the caves. Pockets that had been filled during storms by the giant waves ripping through the D zan Trench. Each time a storm tore through, it continued to fill the pockets of air. That was how two of the caves, here in the trench, became underwater caverns, but now most of their air supply was depleted from all of the fish talk.

Fortunately for them, Froggle happened to spot an air pocket to the right of them. He tapped on Tsunami's helmet, gentle like, so that he did not hurt his ears. He pointed towards the pocket. Slowly, they rose up into the air, both of them taking several deep breaths.

"Maybe we should limit our conversations to hand signals for now. At least until we have reached a larger cavern to breathe in," said Tsunami.

"Yes, that would be better for me too."

As they started to take a final breath before going under again, Tsunami saw something shine from the corner of his eye. "Hold on a second. Froggle, will you please shine the stones above your head once more? I thought that I saw something." Froggle held the stones up. "There it is again," he said as he swam a little closer to a narrow gap between two walls. "Can you see it, Froggle? What is it?" Tsunami asked, with a very curious look in his eyes. "It looks like gold, but what it is, I cannot tell yet."

As he leaned forward to get a better and closer look, his Crystal started to glow. At first, it startled them both. Then Tsunami paddled backwards in the water. Then the gap between the walls also started to glow and open wider. When the light dimmed some, it revealed a weapon of some kind. It obviously belonged to the Guardian before him.

"There is no mention of a weapon like this in the prophecy," Tsunami said.

"So what is it for and why is it here?" Froggle looked around at Tsunami, with his body twisted around.

"Oh, yes, I forgot that you do not know what I am talking about. I will explain it to you some other time. For now though, I am going to get this incredible-looking triton. Not just a plain trident either. No, this weapon has clearly been forged by some godly being."

It was solid gold, with three prongs at the top of it. Each of them had a large hook at their tip. The bar that went up the center was the longest. The hook tip that was on it had four sides to it. The other two bars bowed outward and then up. Both of the tips on them were the same. Each had a single hook on them. Right below the spear-like top was this oval area, about two inches wide and three inches long. There was some cryptic writing on the outer portion, but in the center was what appeared to be a portion of the Elemental Crystal. Finally, right below this, were four little spikes that curved out and then upward.

The Crystal started to glow. It was blue and it illuminated the cave. It looked like a blue diamond. As Tsunami reached for it and picked it up, it started to glow even brighter. The light was so bright that it exited from every opening there was. For a brief moment, it even lit up the trench outside of the cave. When the light dimmed down, there was a new opening in the wall of the cave. Tsunami and Froggle entered through it.

The cavern they entered was an unknown place. There had never been any mention of it before. As they got out of the water, Tsunami noticed another circle containing the symbol of the Water Guardian. Except, this time, the triton which he held leaned itself forward. Tsunami held on tightly and let it do whatever it was that it was doing.

Then, all of a sudden, some low electricity started coming out from the Crystal on the triton to the four spikes that were below it. From there, the electricity grew stronger as it traveled up to the fork at the top. The electricity joined itself around the top of the triton's three sections. Then it sent out a quick blast at the circle.

The whole thing lit up, just like in the castle. The stone began to ripple like the floor did. Then it swirled around, pushing outward until it splashed back in. It transformed itself into an illuminated pool of water on the side of the wall.

Tsunami looked down at Froggle. "Wait here for me. I am going to go into the circle. I must do this alone." Tsunami then jogged over and jumped into the pool.

When he made it to the other side, he found himself swimming to the surface of yet another cavern. Here, it was more of a narrow opening. When he climbed out, it was a small room. On the wall to his left was an indentation of his triton. He took the triton and placed it in its spot. When it was placed in its spot, a box came down from the ceiling. When it opened, there was a big blue diamond glowing in it. When he reached for the stone, it disappeared and reappeared upon his chest armor.

"Wow! I can feel the energy that this Crystal possesses." Then he had a vision of his abilities that he now possessed. After he got a grip on himself again, Tsunami jumped back into the pool. When he came back through to the other side, he landed on his face. He forgot that he entered sideways, so when he came back out, he was looking at the floor.

"Are you okay?" asked Froggle.

"Yes."

Then Froggle hunched over and laughed really hard. "You should have seen yourself. It looked funny when you crashed to the ground." He laughed away.

"So you find that to be amusing, do you?" he asked as he got up and brushed himself off.

Then another portal began to open up from the ceiling. Through it came two other Guardians, who fell into the water. They made a splash that made a small wave break onto the shore where Froggle was laughing. The water crashed right over Froggle's body.

"Ha! Ha! Ha! Who is laughing now?" Tsunami asked with a grin on his face. Froggle stumbled to get to his feet.

The two Guardians emerged from the water. "I did not see that one coming," said Tristan.

"I think it put my flame out," Drake said as he held his hand up and created a fireball. "Nope. Still got it."

Then Tsunami lowered his triton and made the water around them lift them up and onto the little shore. "Who are you," he asked, holding the triton out in front of him.

"Hold on a minute there, big guy," Drake said. "We are your new friends. I am Drake, the Fire Guardian, and this is Tristan, the Land Guardian."

Then Tristan stepped forward. "While you were getting your Crystal, some of our enemies were forming a war party. Now we have two choices here. One, we can go back up through that portal to our new home…"

Then Drake stepped in. "Or we can get the others and show these pieces of crap who we are and what we can do."

"The choice is yours."

Then Froggle scattered around Tsunami and climbed up to his shoulder. "I am called Tsunami."

"Yeah, looking at the size of you, I can see why," Tristan said.

"Please, do not interrupt me again," Tsunami said with a stern voice.

"I am sorry. I did not mean to offend you," Tristan responded as he took a step back.

"That is all right. I forgive you," he said as he smiled at Tristan. "Now, I say that we show these scum who we really are. How many Guardians do we have so far?"

"The whole crew is with us, with the exception of the Wind Guardian," Drake answered.

"Then have them come through and we will get started."

Right then, the Twins poked their heads through the portal. "Did someone say fight?" Shaw asked.

"Come, you two, let us make an everlasting impression here, today," Tristan said to them.

"How will we get to the surface," asked Shayla.

"Leave that to me," said Tsunami. "I will use my powers, with the help of my triton, to generate a force field of air around you."

"Who is your little friend, right there," Shayla asked, pointing to Froggle sitting upon Tsunami's shoulder.

"This is my other new friend. His name is Froggle."

"You are so cute. My name is Shayla and this is my brother, Shaw. We are the Heart Guardians." When they came all of the way through, Shaw was holding Shayla as they floated down to the floor.

Drake took a look at the portal. "Shaw, will you please do me a favor and lift me to the portal? Before we go into battle, I must look at the monitors and see where to hit from."

Shaw looked over at Drake. "Sure."

"Tristan," Drake then said, looking over at him, "Do you want Spex here to help? Or should he stay put?"

Tristan thought for a second. "You might want to have him stay and keep guard."

"Okay then. I will have Drãboon stand watch with him. I am bringing Manjynx with us. Besides, I need Drãboon to keep a watch on Flare for me as well."

Tsunami, who was looking very confused, asked, "Who are Manjynx, Flare, Spex, and Drãboon? Are they more Guardians?"

Shayla then walked up to Tsunami. Looking up at him, she said, "No, they are Drake's and Tristan's pets. Manjynx is the Guardian Dragon of Fire and Flare is an orphaned drake. As for Spex, you will have to ask Tristan about him, and Drãboon is Drake's mystical creature. Drake is the only one who can communicate with Drãboon. You will like Manjynx. He is an awesome creature."

Meanwhile, Drake had already gone back to the palace. "He will be back soon," Tristan said as he looked up at Tsunami. He was a giant compared to everyone else there. "If you want, Froggle is welcome to stay at the palace, along with the others."

"Why thank you! Froggle, maybe it would be a good idea if you were to stay here. It will be safer for you."

"If that is what will make you feel better. Okay, I will go."

Then Tristan asked Shaw to give Froggle a lift up. "Can you introduce him to the others as well please?"

"Yes, I sure will. Come on. Jump on my back and hang on."

Froggle jumped from Tsunami's shoulder and across to Shaw's back. Then they disappeared through the portal.

## Chapter 6
## *The Battle of D zan*

While the Guardians were figuring out how to get out of the cave that they were in, Drake was finishing up at the palace. He had been in there for some time now. Everyone was starting to wonder what was taking him so long.

After a short time, Shaw decided that he would take a look. "I shall be right back. I am going to check on Drake. He should have been back by now."

"Very well, Shaw," Tristan said. "Tell him the air in here grows stale."

"All right. I will tell him," he replied as he flew into the portal. When he reached the other side, he almost crashed into Drake.

"Whoa there, partner. Where are you flying off to in a hurry," Drake asked.

"Oh! Sorry about that, Red."

"What is with the name Red?"

"Well, you know. Being the Fire Guardian and all, I thought that Red seemed logical for your nickname."

"Oh, I see now. Yeah, maybe it might be okay. Then I suppose that I shall call you...the Pink Flyer," he said, smiling at Shaw.

"What! Why would you call me that," he asked as he lowered himself to the ground.

"Well, you know. Seeing as how you can fly and your Crystal is pink and all."

"Okay, I get your point. Sorry, Drake."

"Apology accepted and thank you. So, why have you come back?"

"Oh yes! Everyone was wondering what happened to you."

"I am sorry about that. I shall explain what is going on when we are al together. Now rejoin the others and tell them that I will be with you all in a moment. I need to get Manjynx." Then he turned away.

"Yes, sir."

Drake looked around and found Manjynx and Drāboon. "Here you are. Manjynx, go to the portal room. Drāboon, I need your help, my friend. I just hope that you will be able to help," he said anxiously.

"What is it, Drake? I might be able to help you."

"Can you widen the portal so that Manjynx can fit through?"

"Why yes, I can, as a matter of fact. I can open a portal almost anywhere. I told you, I have many different gifts."

"Can you open one for us on the backside of the island of Polarix?"

"I must go through the portal with you there, first. Then, once I am over there, I will be able to."

Drake then started to make his way back to the others. Drāboon followed close behind. When they finally met up with the others, Drake noticed that the room had gotten quite a bit larger. "I see that you made a few changes while I was gone, eh Tristan?"

"After the youngster told me that you were bringing Manjynx with you, I thought it was going to get crowded. So, I made some small changes. So where is your pet dragon?"

"He will be right here. When he arrives, I shall explain our current plans," Drake said as Manjynx and Drāboon came through the portal. "Okay now. Everyone, listen real good. I have counted three water fleets. Small ones, but nevertheless. Never underestimate your opponent. Also, there are scout ships everywhere around the D zan Trench. They must have picked up on our energy readings when you altered the cave. Lucky for us, I have gotten a hold of Prince Lathius of the Goyans. He has a strike team nearby. It is under the control of Commander Kre l. She and her team will be joining us shortly. Are you all ready for this?"

"Yes," everyone answered at once.

"That is good. Now, although we are still one member short of a full crew, I feel that we can still make an appearance that will be talked about for centuries to come. Drãboon here has the ability to open up a portal for us. He will open one on the backside of Polarix for us. From there, we will surprise them from behind. Hopefully, our Goyan friends will be close behind. Are there any questions?"

"Yes, I have one," said Tsunami. "After we kick their butts all over D zan, can we get a bite to eat? I am getting hungry."

Everyone giggled a little. "Yes, my friend, we can. Now, is everyone ready?"

"Yes."

"Then let us pray to the Powers that Be and ask for strength, speed and grace out there tonight. Drãboon, can you please open the portal now?"

"Yes. Just give me a moment." Then Drãboon closed his eyes and began to concentrate. Next, his body started to illuminate. Drãboon's aura had a red glow to it. Then, in the center of the room, right above the water, opened up a large portal. Through it, you could see the back of the castle. One by one, they passed through it.

Drake and Manjynx were the last to go through. Before they did though, Drake looked down at Drãboon. "Thank you for all of your help, Drãboon. Just keep a watchful eye on the others staying back at the palace."

"I will, Drake. Godspeed and good luck in your first battle," he said to Drake as they flew into the portal.

As they came all the way through, the portal closed behind them. "Okay, everybody listen up," Drake said. "I, as the team's leader, will reveal myself first. Tsunami?"

"Yes, Drake?"

"I want you to create some kind of giant wave that will hide us as we come upon our enemy."

"I would be happy to. It will give me the chance to see what this triton is really capable of doing."

"Twins?"

"Yes, Drake?"

"I want you two to stay close and help Tristan. As a matter of fact, Shayla? Could you become a dragon once more? This way, Tristan can catch a ride with you."

"Sure I can. It would be my pleasure," Shayla said as she took a few steps back and transformed into a fierce-looking dragon.

"Tristan?"

"Yes?"

"Do you have any weapon to use? Seeing how we are on a water planet. Not that there is anything wrong with that," Drake smiled as he glanced at Tsunami.

Then Tristan reached out his arm and placed his hand on a boulder that was near him. The giant rock began to change and a crossbow made of stone appeared from out of the rock. Next, he created arrows for it. "Yes, I do."

"Shaw?" asked Drake.

"Yes, sir."

"You stay by your sister and Tristan. When we get close enough, we will break off. Tsunami and I will travel to the left of the ships. You guys will pass to the right. From here, you will attack. All right then. Let's do this," he said, looking at them one at a time. "Well, no more fun and games. Welcome to your destinies, boys and girl. If we keep straight heads and stick together, we will succeed. Now let's get going and remember, wait until I give the signal to break off."

Then Tsunami held up his triton. It started to glow with a blue light surrounding it. All of a sudden, the water began to rise up like a wall. Tsunami stepped into the water. As the wave began moving, so did Tsunami. He was skiing across the water on his feet.

"That looks like fun," Drake said.

"It is. Maybe you would like me to show you sometime."

"Yeah. Thanks, but no thanks. I like it right up here. Besides, I don't think that water spots will look good on my suit."

"Aww! You are full, my friend."

"Maybe so," Drake said, then laughed. "Maybe so." Then Drake looked behind his back at the Twins and Tristan. "We are getting close, so be ready for me to give the signal."

"Yes, sir," they all answered.
"Tsunami. Are you ready to make fish food out of these guys yet?"
"Very funny."
"Sorry. No pun intended."
"I am ready."
Then, just as Drake was going to give his command to attack, the Goyan backup came down from the sky. There were about thirty or so fighter ships that came down behind them.

\* \* \*

Looking off one of the enemy battleships, were a couple of look-out crew men. They noticed the air attack coming. "Hey, look at that in the water," one of them said.
"Forget about the water, man. Sound the alarms! There is an air raid coming," the other crewman shouted and panicked.
"Really! Look in the water. What the heck is that thing?"
After sounding the alarms, the other crewman picked up his binoculars and said, "What the heck are you talking about, man?"
"Let me take a look. What the...? It looks like a giant wave coming right for us. Run and tell the captain to take a look."
"Right," he said and took off into the ship.
The crewman took another look through his binoculars. The next thing that he saw startled him and sent chills down his back. What could have startled him so bad? He saw the Guardians reveal themselves from behind the wave. It was no time at all before an all out battle took place in the sky above, while the Guardians fought in the water. Drake and Manjynx came up and out from behind the wave. Tristan and the Twins followed beside him and Tsunami kept going forward.
"You guys break off and take the ships on the right," Drake shouted.
All of a sudden, the battle ship began to fire their energy cannons upon the Guardians.
"Drake," shouted Tristan. "Take out their weapon room. I have an idea. Cover me."

"What are you going to do?"

"You will see. Shayla, do you see that tiny piece of land emerged from the trench peak?"

"The one in front of us, coming up?"

"Yes. There are about six ships surrounding it."

"Yes. What about it?"

"Take me to it if you would. I want to try something."

"We are on our way."

They swooped down, avoiding getting hit by four energy blasts that came real close. Tristan jumped off of Shayla. He fell about twenty-five feet down and landed on his feet. He came to a crouch and placed one hand on the ground. Then he stood up and raised his arms up, high into the air. The ground began to tremble and the water started to bubble. Then, all at the same time, four huge spikes came ripping up through the center of the ships. The rock tore through everything in its path.

"Yeah," Tristan shouted.

"All right," shouted Shaw, as he flew up to another ship that was close by. He fired his crossbow and the arrows had highly explosive tips on them. He managed to destroy their weapons station, while Shayla flew down and hovered above it, blasting it with flames, torching them one at a time.

In another area, Tsunami hit three more ships with his giant wave. There were ships going down all over the place. In the air, the battle lit up the sky. Both the enemy fighters and the Goyan fighters were getting hit. Unfortunate for the enemy of course because our guys were kicking butt everywhere.

A scout ship was heading right towards Tristan. It was coming up behind him. Shayla noticed it and then swooped down from the sky to pick him up. The enemy began firing at them, as Tristan jumped on Shayla's back. They were misses. Then, from the side, Tsunami stood on top of the water and using his triton, he made a funnel of water blast up and hit the scout ship, launching it into the ocean.

Meanwhile, Shaw was heading towards one of the ships. He was being fired upon by some gunmen on the ship. He kept dodging their energy weapon blasts. He flew right over the top of them. As he started to turn around, one of the gunmen got off a lucky shot, that hit Shaw. There was a small explosion. The other Guardians stared in awe.

Shayla cried out, "Shaw, no!" as he fell into the ocean below him. As Shayla passed the ship, the enemy fired upon her too. She took a deep breath and let out a huge flame. It was a direct hit to the gunmen on the ship.

Right then, Shaw burst out of the ocean. "Woo-hoo!" Then he flew straight up into the air and stopped. He took a good look at the ship and dove straight down on it.

"What is he doing now?" asked Shayla.

"Just wait and see," Tristan said.

Then they watched as Shaw crashed right through the center of the ship and into the water. There was an explosion and Shaw burst back up out of the water. The enemy started pouring out from the ship and started jumping into the ocean. The ship exploded and began to sink. "Yeah! Who wants to be next?"

"Good job, kid," Tsunami shouted as he made the water rise up around another ship. Then, with his triton in hand, he pointed it towards the ship and froze the water, trapping it so that it couldn't go anywhere.

"That was good thinking, Tsunami," Drake said as he and Manjynx turned sharp to avoid being hit by an energy blast. "I have an idea," he told Manjynx. "Try to come up next to that scout ship, to the left of us. Get as close to it as you can, Manjynx." As they approached the scout ship, Drake said something to Manjynx. "I am going to jump off of you, my friend. I want you to fly down and catch me." As he got close to enough to his target, he jumped through the air. The next thing that happened caught the attention of a lot of people. Drake did a flip over the top of the scout ship. In the process of it, out of nowhere, he pulled out a long sword made of flames. As he passed over, he took the sword of fire and sliced the craft right in half. Then, as he fell towards the ocean, Manjynx swooped by and caught him on his back. It was an awesome sight to see.

"How did you do that?" Shaw asked. "That was so cool."

Drake nodded. "I will tell you later. Keep yourself focused on what you are doing."

The battle continued for a little while longer. "They are leaving," Shayla shouted out, with Tristan still riding on her back.

"Yes. They are retreating. We have won this battle," Tristan said.

Then, all of them headed back to Polarix, where they met up with Commander Kre l and her team. Shayla and Tristan came down softly. After Tristan jumped down from her back, Shayla transformed back into herself.

"You guys have to see this," Shayla said to the crew. "Tristan, will you please show them all what you can do? It is so cool!" Shayla seemed to be very excited about something.

"All right already," he said, and he shook his head, smiling.

Commander Kre l walked up to Drake from the side. He looked over at her and he smiled. "Commander Kre l, I presume."

"Yes, and you are obviously the Fire Guardian."

"You can call me Drake."

"All right, Drake. What is going on here?"

"Tristan is about to show us something," he said, loud enough for everyone to hear.

"Yes, I am getting ready to do a little trick. You must be Commander Kre l. I am Tristan, the Land Guardian. It would seem that you are just in time for my performance."

"It is nice to meet you."

"I am Shayla. This is my brother Shaw and he is Tsunami," she said as she pointed at Tsunami.

"It is very nice to meet you all."

"Well, yes. Now then," said Tristan. "Here I go." As he stood there with his legs apart and arms out, but pointing down, he began to change. His feet and legs changed first. Then, slowly up his entire body, he turned into the gravel in which he stood upon. Then his body sank into the ground.

"Where did he go?" Tsunami asked.

"I don't know," Shaw said with a surprised look upon his face.

No one could see Tristan, but he could see everyone else as he traveled undetected through the ground. All of the sudden, right behind Drake and the commander, he started to rise from the ground. When he was up completely, his body began to change back. "Hello! It is nice to meet you," he said.

They both jumped a tiny bit. "Where did you come from? How did you do that?" Commander Kre l asked.

"It is one of my perks, being the Land Guardian and all. Of course I have heard what Drake can do is pretty cool too. Or should I say hot?"

Then Commander Kre l looked at Drake. "Oh yeah? And what can you do?"

"I do not know. What can I do, Tristan?" He looked at him.

"The Twins say that you told them something about lava."

"Ah, yes. I can walk on lava without sinking or burning up."

"That is pretty hot. Now, I am sorry to be rude, but I must be getting along soon," Commander Kre l said.

"No, we are the ones who should say sorry. I wanted to say on behalf of the Guardians, minus one for now, thank you and your team very much for helping us out there. Who knows how it would have turned out if you did not make it when you did," Drake said.

"You are quite welcome, Guardians," Commander Kre l said as she smiled.

"Maybe you and your team could stay for dinner. I will fix us all a great big feast," said Tsunami. "The D zan sharks are very tasty."

"Thank you, but I am sorry, we cannot. Maybe soon though."

"All right then. Until next time, be safe and enjoy life," said Tsunami.

"Thank you all again. By the way, you all can call me Alexis," she said, then turned around and walked away.

Everyone then shouted out, "Good bye!"

Shayla walked up to Drake. "A-hem! Excuse me, you guys. She is very pretty, don't you think?"

"Oh! Ah, yes, she is," Drake said in a subtle voice.

"Yeah. You are right about that," Tristan answered as well.

"How about you, Tsunami? Do you think that she is pretty also?" Shayla asked.

He took a short breath. "She is almost as pretty as you are. Nevertheless, neither of you are my type."

"Why thank you, Tsunami. That was a very nice thing to say," Shayla said as she started to blush. "You might look scary, but I like you, and not just because you said that either. I can just tell. Call it intuition."

Shaw walked over to where his sister was. "Yeah! Yeah! It is a girl thing. I just think that you're really awesome. I think that all of you guys are awesome. By the way, Mr. Drake, how did you make that sword of fire out there? That was so cool. How did you cut that scout ship right in half?" Shaw seemed to be really excited about the battle and Drake's fight.

"Okay. I will tell you now. It was pretty easy, actually. All I did was think, *If I can control the element of fire, maybe I could use it as an actual weapon.* Then I said, 'Give me a sword of fire and make it real hot.' Next thing I know, I touched my hands to my chest and pulled out this flaming sword of fire. When I finished using it, it vanished back into my Crystal. I bet that Tristan and Tsunami could do the same with theirs."

Shayla and Shaw asked them to try, but Tsunami told them, "Later. For now, we eat. Who will help me catch dinner," Tsunami asked.

Right about then, Drake called out to them, "Wait a minute, guys and girl. Don't run off just yet. Tsunami, I am sorry about this. I know that you are hungry, but can you hold on for a few more minutes?"

Tsunami stopped and turned to listen, as did the Twins. "Yes? I am listening," said Tsunami. Then his stomach gave out a loud growl. It was so loud that Shayla jumped off to the side and Shaw jumped into the air.

"What was that?" asked Shaw.

"Sorry, that was my stomach. It has been four days since my last meal. I eat until I fill up, then I eat no more until it is time. Now, what is it that you wanted to say?"

"I was just going to say that if you can hold on, we must get back to the palace. There is plenty of food there. We prepared for your arrival and the Twins went out with the companions of ours to find some food for you. I must get back and get a hold of Lord Lathius or the Emperor himself. I have to tell him how everything went. Maybe you should all join me, to tell him, or them, our gratitude to them for sending help quickly. Then we can all celebrate and feast."

# Story 5

# Chapter 1
# Whisper

After their celebration, the Guardians all joined the families back at their homes, at least for a few days, by order of Drake. He, on the other hand, just wanted to take some time to finally mourn. This way, he would be able to get some closure for himself. Well, that and restore some of his home. In the meantime, we journey to Kel-Terra, where we will begin our final story to this new saga that lies ahead.

\* \* \*

We find our Wind Guardian to be somewhere on the Henna Moon. This was a very beautiful moon. Although small in size compared to its sister moons Talaron 3 and Talaron 6, it was definitely the most beautiful of the three. With awesome landscapes and the most beautiful sunsets in the known system, it had one flaw. That was due to the passing of the other two moons. They cast their shadows upon Henna, which caused hot and cold fronts. This made the moon very windy at times.

Fortunately for the beings who lived here, they could fly. They were a special race of beings who lived here. Only larger space crafts could even enter the moon's atmosphere. These divine creatures, who looked like angels, stood about seven feet tall and were physically fit in every way. They had a wingspan of around twelve feet across and two and one half feet wide. They were the only creatures alive, other than a full-grown dragon, that could survive the wind's powerful forces. So far, all other who tried failed.

Carak I Bay ran along the Carak I Cliffs. The cliffs were about one and a half miles high from the ground sea level. With narrow canyons and greenery all around, the winds were unpredictable, which made it a hard place to live. At the same time though, it was the perfect place to hide the Element of Wind. Only a special, chosen being could make it through these lands alive.

As the wind picked up and the sun began to set, we find our Guardian to be sitting atop of the canyon, along its plains. Lined up along the edges of the narrow canyon openings were very large trees all intertwined together with houses built in them. They were built just under the top branches. This kept them hidden from passersby. It also provided shade from the two suns' harmful rays, which could take a toll on one's feathers.

"Whisper," a voice called out from behind the Guardian.

"Yes, my brother? What is it?" she asked as she turned and stretched her wings open.

"How come you have to go away? No one can fly down through the canyon. Not this one that you must travel in."

"It will be okay, Serrat. It is my destiny. Remember what we were told in the stories when we were growing up? Only a chosen being will make the journey through this place. The Elemental Being."

"Do not take me the wrong way, my sister. I know you will make it. It is just that you are my sister and I worry about you."

"Yes, I understand. That is one of the reasons that I love you so much. You always look out for me, when it should be me who is looking out for you," Whisper said, then walked over to her brother and gave him a hug. "The sunset is beautiful tonight, Serrat," she said while stepping away from her brother. "I must be going. Please tell Mother good-bye for me. It has been hard enough on her after Father's accidental death. You know how she feels about the canyon already."

"It will be fine, Whisper. Do not worry about it," he cut in on her. "I will look after Mother. You just go and come back a Guardian. I am proud of you, Whisper. I know that you will be a great Guardian. I also know that you will be back soon. Now, go before I change my mind and panic. Just kidding," he said as he gave her another hug. Then he kissed her on the right cheek.

"What was that for?"

"It was for luck. Not that you needed it, but nevertheless." Then Serrat turned and flew away, back towards his home.

Then, as Whisper looked down into the treacherous canyon below, she thought, *Father, if you can hear me, please look over Mother and Serrat for me. I will be fine. I know it. Something inside keeps telling me that everything will be fine for me. So I ask you to look out for them.* After she finished her thought, she jumped off of the cliffside and opened her wings. With her head arched forward, she brought her wings in closer and shot through the sky like a falling star.

## Chapter 2
## *Finding a Key to the Past*

While cutting through the winds, Whisper realized that her helmet, which she had received from Emperor Miethius, kept her face shielded very well. Not only that, it allowed her to focus better on the objects around her. The surroundings that she was flying into seemed all too familiar to her.

*This narrow canyon looks just like it does in my dreams,* Whisper thought as she kept looking around. Fighting to get through some of the stronger winds and pulling off the bends and edges of the cliffs all around her was a challenge in itself. The uncontrollable winds carried debris through here all of the time. This just meant that she had to be even more careful than if she was on higher grounds.

As time passed and the weather grew colder, Whisper noticed that her view through the helmet remained the same. Even though her species could see great distances during the day and it improved greatly at night, the twilight hours were hazy. It was during this time of day that her father met his accidental fate. This unique new helmet provided a lens which filtered out the sun's blinding rays. It actually allowed her to see clearly during this time of day for the first time.

Suddenly, from the corner of her left side, she noticed a sparkle coming from the rocks, so she flew towards it. When she landed, the spot that she was standing in seemed to not be as windy. She looked around for the sparkle that caught her eye. As she bent over to look behind a large boulder, she saw the sparkle again. It came from the right side, next to her. She brushed a few rocks off to the side and picked up the object. Whisper fell to her knees. It was her father's bracelet. The one that she and her brother gave him, shortly before he died. She began to cry for a moment before she took off her helmet to wipe her face.

"Oh, Daddy. I miss you so much. Mother has been heartbroken without you here. She is a strong woman though. She keeps her head high and keeps going on. Serrat has become a good man, like you, Father. You would be very proud of him," Whisper said to herself in a soft voice. "I miss you! I will make you proud of me too, Father. Until the afterlife, Father. I love you, wherever you may be." Then she placed the bracelet on her own wrist, put her helmet back on, and held up her chin. "Now to find an entrance somewhere."

As she flew on, she was looking for anything else that might have belonged to her father. His name was Rhudaki. He was a strong figure amongst the people. Not only as a figure head, but as a man as well.

One late afternoon, while bringing dinner home, he misjudged his distance to the barrier that separated from the canyon winds from pulling someone or something into its grasp. It was during the blinding time that this happened. Before Rhudaki could react, it was too late. The winds had grabbed a hold of him and pulled him right in. It was a great tragedy amongst the land. Beings came from the farther regions to mourn for his death. Now, Whisper must come to terms with herself in order to move on and be at her best, for she was the chosen one. With her head held high, she continued on, looking for a sign or something that might catch her eyes.

After about ten minutes passed, something up ahead looked as though it flew across the canyon. *How could this be?* she wondered. *I thought nothing could survive down here.* Then Whisper flew faster towards the location of the object that she had seen. There was nothing around, but a noise was coming from behind her. As she turned around to see what it was, it was gone. "Am I hearing and seeing things now?"

*Swoosh!* Again, the sound came from behind her. This time, when she turned, she saw a little winged creature duck behind a boulder, off to the right of the canyon walls. Whisper shot towards it as fast as she could. "There you are," she said as she looked around the boulder, but no one was there. "Okay, what is going on here? Either this creature is really fast or I'm going nuts. Which is it?"

She started to turn around again to keep moving on. "Oh! Awe…what the…don't do that to me," she shouted, as she fell back on her butt. She was startled, for there was this little creature flying stationary in front of her. "What are you? Can you talk? Where did you come from, I wonder."

The little creature looked somewhat like a cross between a miniature man with a hawk, from the waist down, and a small hint of a dragon also. The wings resembled that of a dragon's wings, plus it has a tail. Its tail was long and it narrowed as it came to its end. Down the center of its back, there were short but strong spikes. At the tips, they were split and each of the ends contained a spike with a slight hook to them. This looked like it would help with hunting and holding on to something. The creature itself was no more than twelve or thirteen inches high. Yet, they could withstand the winds down here and they were very fast too, but what were they? To Whisper, this creature and others like it were unknown around here.

Then, just as quick as it appeared, it disappeared. It flew off real fast, but not too fast that Whisper could not see where it went. She saw it fly towards something around the corner of the canyon walls about a half of a mile up ahead, so she followed it. When she caught up to where it had flown, it was perched upon a ridge in the cliff. "Well! You really are a fast little guy, that is for sure," she said as she moved a little closer to him. "I won't hurt you. I just want to try to find a way to talk to you. Please do not be afraid of…"

Before she could finish, the creature smiled at her and leaped off of his perch. "Not again. I don't know if he is playing with me or trying to tell me something. I do wonder if there are more of them and why haven't they ever been seen before now. There is so much I would like to know about this creature, but I must stay focused on my goals

## THE GUARDIANS OF ZENULAR

first. I had better start looking for my symbol or sign and worry about my little friend later."

Then she jumped into the air and continued to move on, looking up and down the canyon for anything at all. Suddenly, up in the distance, there was a curve in the side of the canyon, which was strange looking. Whisper was nearly halfway through the canyon. It was at this center point that the curve began. That is why she thought it to be so strange. As she came closer to it, she noticed that the winds began to calm somewhat rapidly. Then they died out completely when she reached the center. About twenty feet above her, the winds continued to blow.

"This is the sign I have been waiting for."

The entrance to the curve in the canyon wall was more like a dome shape. It went inwards about twenty-five feet, then it rounded off in an inverted sort of way, tapered up. Thus, hiding it from the world above. That was why it had not been seen from above. Besides that, the way that the light bent off of the walls also created the illusion that nothing was there. Down where Whisper now was, on the other hand, there were hieroglyphs on the walls of the entrance. They were pictures of what looked like a group of those little creatures, standing and flying around a Wind Guardian. She was letting them sit on her shoulder even.

"That creature must have been trying to show me this place." As she looked on, she noticed a symbol on the flat wall in front of her. It bore the mark of the Wind Guardian and it contained a place to set her guidance Crystal.

In order to make herself stronger, Whisper only used her guidance Crystal when she could not come to a solution on her own. This not only made her more independent as a being, but it strengthened her mind skills as well. She had always been a thinker and doer. Maybe it had to do with part of being a chosen one. Then again, maybe not.

She took her Crystal and placed it into the setting. The Crystal began to glow. Then the symbol illuminated as well. Suddenly, the stone wall began to blow inward in little pieces, as though it was blowing away like a sand castle in the wind. It opened a doorway to a cavern within the canyon wall. Whisper's Crystal stayed afloat in the air, so she took it in hand and entered the cavern. When she was in all the way, she just stood there for a moment and looked around, amazed by the sight she was seeing in front of her. It was like a different world altogether. In fact, you could probably say that it was a world within a world.

The cavern was quite large, with openings all over the place. Crystals illuminated the entire inside walls, almost as if they were placed here. Sunlight also shone in from cracks in the canyon walls, providing light to most of the upper portions of the walls. There were also Crystals that hung from some of the smaller holes, which reflected light from the suns as well. And yet the most amazing thing of all was that there were miniature homes and buildings, built all around. It was a civilization designed for these creatures like the one Whisper had seen earlier.

Everything seemed to be empty, but there were no signs of any trouble anywhere. Then came a noise from behind one of the stone houses. The city in the caverns was primitive, which also meant they could be fragile. So Whisper carefully leaped up and flew over the house to investigate the noise. When she reached it, the little creature she had seen earlier was standing there, smiling at her.

"Oh! It's you. I was wondering what happened to you." The creature then flew up to the top of the roof on the house. Whisper then landed on the ground beside him. "Are you here all by yourself?"

He shook his head no.

"Then you can understand me, can't you?"

He nodded yes.

"Can you speak?"

He shook his head no.

"I guess 'yes or no' questions and answers will do then. Do you know where the others are at?"

He nodded and grabbed her by the hand, and gave it a little pull.

"I guess you want me to go somewhere with you," she asked as they flew up to a cave tunnel just up ahead. They entered the tunnel, which was actually pretty wide. "Where are we going," she asked, knowing he could not answer.

## THE GUARDIANS OF ZENULAR

They came to a dead end. The creature touched the wall and it began to separate. When it stopped, it made an opening, just large enough for Whisper to walk through, as long as she tucked her wings in. They entered a chamber. It was also quite large and rounded with a dome at the top. "This looks like the inside of Dome Peak, right by Carak l Bay." There were little openings circling the room, but none of them opened to the outside. In the center of the floor was a giant symbol of the Wind Guardian.

She walked to the center of the floor and looked around. All of the sudden, emerging from every hole, was one of these creatures. They all stared down at Whisper. She was amazed at the sight of how many there were before her. The creature that brought her to the chamber then flew up to an empty space left for him. The next thing that happened was even more amazing. All of these creatures that could not speak started to hum. The sounds coming from their mouths were the most beautiful sounds that Whisper had ever heard. It sounded like a divine melody.

Then, right underneath her, the floor symbol began to glow. Light came up from the symbol all around her. Like Sprite Dust, it ascended up to the center top of the dome. There was a very large Crystal hanging down. It was emerging from the rock ceiling and consuming the light, making it glow brighter. Once it reached it brightest point, Whisper's Crystal began to glow bright. Then a beam shot out of it, straight at the Crystal above. The light became too intense for everyone to look at, so they turned away from it. Then, as the light dimmed, a body began to descend from the Crystal. It was the first Wind Guardian. A celestial being, more divine than any other Guardian ever.

As she floated down to the floor to stand in front of Whisper, who was down on one knee and bowing before her, she said, "Rise, my child. You need not bow before me." Then she reached out for Whisper's hand. As she helped her to her feet, she smiled. "I am Tara Chyme, and you are Whisper. Is that right?"

"Yes, I am, but how did you know my name?" asked Whisper with a curious set of eyes.

"I know a lot, my dear. I am also an Oracle, but soon it will be another's job. I am getting too old to keep on going."

"Will I be the Oracle now?"

"No, dear, I am afraid you will not be the one. In fact, the next to become Oracle is a boy."

"How can that be? I thought that Oracles were supposed to be female only," Whisper said, confused about the situation.

"Yes, they are generally female, but once in a millennium, if this child is male, then he will inherit the gift of the Oracle and he will be great. Although I cannot tell you his name, I can say this. You will soon meet him and when you do, you will know."

"How will I know?"

"You will just know. Now, to do what it is I am here for." Then Chyme placed her hand upon Whisper's head and closed her eyes. The aura that circled them began to glow. It only took but a brief moment for all of the powers of the Guardian to transfer from Chyme to Whisper.

When it was over, Whisper opened her eyes. She did not see the same beautiful being in front of her, but a crone instead. A fragile, old woman was now before her. "Chyme? Is that you?"

"I am afraid so, my dear. Now that you have obtained the powers of the Zenular Wind Element, it's time for me to rest," she said as she slumped over, too old to even hold up her body because of her wings. "Now it is your turn to bring back peace to the planets. Before I go, there is one thing that I wish to show you."

"What is that, Chyme?"

"I want you to turn around and look by the door," she said, pointing towards the entrance.

As Whisper turned around to look, there was a group of the creatures covering the doorway. "What are these creatures called?"

"They are called Hawkois. They will help you with building things or whatever else they can. They are very loyal creatures and friendly to beings who are good within. Now watch!"

Suddenly, one by one, they uncovered the doorway, from the bottom up until they revealed...

"Oh my goodness. Is that really him?" Whisper asked as she stared at the being in front of her. "Daddy!" she cried out. "Daddy, you're alive!"

"Yes, my love. I have been trapped down here waiting for the day you would come," he answered with cheerfulness in his voice.

Then Chyme started to glow. Both Whisper and her father turned to look as they embraced each other with a big hug. "Well, my job is done here. Now I must leave you both. Good luck in your journeys that lie ahead. You will do fine as long as you stay true to yourself."

"Thank you. Thanks for bringing me my father back alive."

"Do not thank me. Thank the Hawkois, for they found your father," said Chyme as she vanished into thin air.

"Thank you, little friends. I will be forever grateful to you. I will tell no one about your existence here. This way, you will not be bothered, but for now, we must go. I have my father to bring home and some friends to meet."

Just then, the same creature that showed Whisper the way stood on a rock before her. "Now that you have become the Guardian, you will also be able to understand us. Only the Guardian of Wind shall be able to understand us. Chyme has made this possible for you." The creature then crouched down as though he was getting ready to fly away. "My name is Eton. If you ever need us, just call and we will awaken for you."

"Thank you, Eton."

"Yes, thank you for looking out and caring for me all of this time," said her father, Rhudaki.

"You are quite welcome, he says, Daddy."

Then he leaped up and joined the others.

"Well, let's get you home. Everyone will be so happy to see you. Especially Mother and Serrat." With that, they set out to get back home.

## Chapter 3
## *The Reunion of a Lifetime*

After talking together for a while, Whisper and her father, Rhudaki, were near the entrance of the caverns, where they would soon be going back out into the winds. Rhudaki had not seen the outside world for several years now. At least both of the suns had set and it was now nighttime. Whisper raised her hand and the door opened just as before. It began to crumble open.
"Here we go, Daddy. I'm taking you home." Whisper was so happy to see her father alive that she could not stop crying.
"I have missed you too, my dear. I wish to hold on for a moment though."
"Sure, we can wait for a moment, but what is it?"
"I know that you are the Guardian, but I almost died in these winds. Are you sure you can do this?"
"Don't worry about these winds, Father. Just watch and see." Whisper closed her eyes and tilted her head back. Extending her arms away from her body, she commanded the winds to slow down to a near stop. This was the first time in over a millennium that the winds had even changed at all.
"You truly can control the winds. Maybe you could have them carry your old dad up to our home." Rhudaki just smiled at Whisper and stared at her.

"No worries, Daddy. Just sit back and watch the beginner at work. Ha, ha! I bet you thought I was going to say pro, didn't you?" She smiled back at her father.

"Well, let me see what you can do. Impress me with your new powers."

"I shall give it my best. Hey, wait just a moment. Are you saying that what I just did wasn't impressive enough?"

"No. Not at all, my dear. I just wanted to be taken home the easy way. You know, with not flying for so long."

"Okay, okay. I guess I can help my poor old father get along. Shall I fly up to the top and get you a walker too, old man?"

"Hey now. Watch that old talk there. I can still handle my own, I will have you know."

"I believe it. You were always quite a strong man. We should be going now though. I want to get you home." Then she held her father by his hand and they leaped up into the night sky. As they got about halfway up the canyon, Whisper looked at her father. "You had better hold tight, Daddy. We are about to see how fast I can fly through the air now," she shouted as they began to accelerate at speeds of one hundred miles per hour, plus. Whisper's heart began to race, as did her father's. She noticed that they were getting closer to home, so she slowed way down. Her father let go of her hand and continued to fly on his own.

There were torches lit up everywhere. Apparently everyone was amazed by this change of the winds. They waited anxiously for the return of Whisper.

"Mother. Come see this. The canyon winds have slowed to a whisper. She has done it. Mother."

"Yes, child. I am coming. Try not to ruffle your feathers up now, Serrat. I'm sure you sister will be home soon, if she has indeed achieved her destiny," Whisper's mother said. All of the sudden her jaw dropped open and her eyes opened wide. She had a look of confusion and hope in her eyes.

"What is it, Mother?" Serrat asked as he turned to see what it was his mother was so entranced by. As he turned half circle, Whisper and her father were setting foot down in front of him. "Father."

"Rhudaki. Is it really you?"

They both came forward to embrace, both Whisper and Rhudaki. "Yes, my love. It is me. I have been trapped down in the canyon this entire time. The winds were too strong to fight, but our daughter has found me and brought me home."

Everyone was so happy and thankful for Rhudaki's return home. They were all in tears, from the joy of him still being alive. He was the first of his kind to ever survive such a brutal fall. It was a miracle.

"Everyone come see. My daughter Whisper has become the Wind Guardian. She has also brought home her father, Rhudaki," shouted out Bella-Yari. "He is alive! Everyone come see!" Then she embraced him again, expressing her joy, thanking her daughter for returning with her father. Of course she was also happy for her daughter's safe return. Bella-Yari feared that her daughter might suffer the same fate as her father, not knowing that he was still alive.

As the entire village began to gather around, Serrat pulled his sister, Whisper, off to the side. "Whisper, please come with me for a moment, to the backroom."

"Sure, Serrat. What is it? You look pale and worried about something," she said to him as he fell into a trance. "Serrat, what is happening to you?"

Then he started to talk. "You must go. Hurry though."

"What are you talking about, Serrat? Go where?" she asked with a real confused look upon her face.

"To the other side of the canyon, across from us. A child who cannot yet fly is about to fall."

"How do you know tha... No way, it cannot be."

"You must go now, Whisper."

Right then, a mother cried out, "My baby! Where is my son? Talon, where are you?" the mother started to panic.

"There he is, on the other side," a man shouted out.

Just as Whisper ran out the door and leaped from the porch, the child began to fall. "Oh no! I had better move quick." As she reached out to save the little boy, a branch growing out of the canyon wall started to move. "What? Am I seeing things or did that branch move?"

As the child fell towards the branch, it started growing up and out of the wall. The child landed right into the tree branch. Everyone watching, including Whisper, stopped to watch in amazement as the branch took the boy all the way back up to his mother. Then it crumbled into dust. Whisper flew back towards everyone. All of the sudden, the ground began to move in a small area near the boy and his mother. Up from the ground came the shape of a being, starting to take shape.

Within seconds, Tristan had emerged. "You should be more careful next time, little one. At least wait until you can fly."

"Thank you, kind sir. How can I ever repay you?"

"I am looking for the being called Whisper."

"Look behind you, stranger."

Tristan turned to see who was behind him. "Well, now I know why they say the Wind Guardian is a divine creature," Tristan said in a soft voice.

Whisper landed on the ground next to Tristan. "I take it you are the Land Guardian? How did you get here? Very few beings have ever been able to withstand the winds on our moon."

"I came through the portal that opens a passage from our headquarters to the bay just beyond those canyon walls. I am the only one who could stay grounded here long enough to find you."

"Was that supposed to be a joke? You know, being the Land Guardian?"

"Yeah, well, I guess my humor could use a little help, but at least you picked up on it."

"You are right. You can use a little help. So are you going to show us what you really look like?" Whisper asked as she removed her helmet.

"Oh! Yes, I'm sorry. Here, let me take off my helmet. There, is this better?"

"Yes, thank you. I prefer to talk face to face with you. Perhaps you could lift yourself up to be at eye level with me," Whisper said, smiling at Tristan.

"Now who is being funny? Was that supposed to be a joke?"

"Okay. So I will work on my humor too. So tell me, Tristan, what brings you here right now?"

"I have been sent here to escort you to our new home, on Craixe. Drake, he is the Fire Guardian and our team leader, asked me to show you the way to your new life. Just so you know, you can come back at any time. The portal opens from both sides. I will show you how to open it, okay?" She nodded yes. "I will let you say good-bye to your family now." He moved to the side to let her pass.

"Serrat," she said as she remembered what he had said to her. "Tristan?"

"Yes, Whisper? What is it? Is there something wrong?"

"Well, no and yes. It is hard to explain."

"Try me."

"Okay. It's like this. When I was given my powers by my predecessor, she mentioned to me that I should look out for a boy who would become Oracle. I think it is my little brother, Serrat. Before the accident that just passed, he...he told me it was going to happen. To hurry."

"What," Tristan said with surprise in his voice. "If this is true, we will have to bring him with us too."

"I can't. My mother and father would be heartbroken all over again. This time because they would be all alone."

"I'll tell you what. You go and visit with your family for a few and I will see what I can do about this situation. Will that be all right with you?"

"Yes. Thank you. When you are ready, just come into my house."

"I will."

Whisper then flew up to the porch. Tristan got on his communicator and got a hold of Drake.

While they are both busy doing what needs to be done, we shall take a look at what the enemy has in store.

## Chapter 4
## *The Unity Is Complete*

A strand of short events were about to take place and a unity was about to be completed. After talking to Drake and waiting for his response, it was decided that Bella-Yari and Rhudaki could stay with Lexia and Tork at the castle. At least it would help keep them occupied while their children were away. Serrat had been taken to the Guardians' palace, where he would be kept safe. There, he could safely develop his skills as Oracle, while his sister stayed behind to say good-bye to her mother and father, who were packing their things. She would also restore the powerful winds that protected the entrance of her new friends' lair. The rest of the Guardians were called back to the palace, where they would prepare for war against General Ney-Glom's army. Prince Lathius had informed the Guardians that Goyan was attacked earlier by several energy bombs sent from near ships that had since retreated. It was a warning of what was to come.

Back at Valladamier's hideout, Major Bax had just delivered a package to the Emperor himself. It contained a scroll of some type of ancient writing. Major Bax had been asked to stay behind and assemble a team to decipher the ancient writings in the scroll. Meanwhile, Valladamier had plans of his own to deal with.

Once again, as the events began to thicken, our story unfolds. So with this in mind, let us continue and see what will happen next.

Back on the Henna Moon, Whisper was saying her good-byes for now. "Mother...Father..." Whisper said, realizing that she was too old to be saying "Daddy" much longer. "First I want you to both know that I promise to keep Serrat as safe as possible. Next, I love you both. You will both be safe at the Aleagra Castle and do not worry, we will be by to visit all the time. I will also see if it is possible to have you guys over at the palace."

"It is going to be fine, my dear," Rhudaki said with a smile.

"Yes. Your father is right. Somehow, we just know that everything will be fine." Bella-Yari then reached out and gave Whisper a big hug. "My beautiful daughter. You have always been a strong person. I have no doubt that you will be one of the best Guardians ever. I love you, Whisper. Take care of Serrat and tell him to call me on his communicator please." Then she whispered into her daughter's ear, "Thank you for everything."

"Whisper," Rhudaki said in a humble manner.

"Yes, Father?"

"Perhaps you should get going. It is getting late in the night."

"Yes, perhaps you are right. Oh, before I go, here is your bracelet back. I found it in the canyon."

"Thank you. I thought that I had lost it forever." Rhudaki paused for a moment. "Here. I want you to hold on to it for me. Keep it for luck. This way, I know it is safe."

"All right then. I will keep it for luck then." She smiled and placed it on her wrist. "I am so happy to have you here alive with us once again. I love you too." She gave them both hugs and kisses. "I must go now. I will check in on you later, to see how you like the castle." With that said, she flew off to meet Tristan at the portal. "Tristan. I am ready to join you at the site you mentioned." She called him on the communicator he had left for her.

"All right. Give me just a moment and I will open the portal for you."

Whisper headed for Carak I Bay. As she made her way there, she took a look around. *I am going to miss this place,* she thought. When she reached the bay, Tristan was already there waiting for her.

"Well, glad you could make it."

"Yes! Well, at least this will be a great learning experience for all of us."

"I bet no one would argue with that. This will be a learning experience, plus we have awesome armor suits and powers too boot. Could you ask for anything better than that?"

They paused for a moment. "Okay, I am ready now."

"All right then. After you." Tristan bowed, then motioned his arms for Whisper to pass through the portal to her new life and home.

Although she would be living at the palace, she knew that Henna was really home to her. At least she wouldn't be alone here, because just on the other side of the portal, her brother, Serrat, awaited her arrival.

"It's about time. I have been waiting for you. Come with me. You have got to see this place. Oh, that is if you are not busy already," he said as he tucked in his wings and stared up at his sister.

Whisper smiled at him. Tristan stepped forward and cut in. "I think that would be a wonderful idea. Why don't you take her out to meet everyone and show your sister around?" Then he turned to Whisper. "This will also give me a chance to see what is going on with our current situation on Goyan."

"Shouldn't I help with that?"

"Later. After all of the details have been worked out. Then Drake and I will get everyone together."

"Who's Drake?"

Then a voice came from behind her. "That would be me."

"He's the Fire Guardian," Serrat whispered to his sister.

"Thank you. I can see that."

Drake made his way towards Whisper with his arm extended in greeting. "Hello. If you don't mind me saying, you're beautiful. I had no idea." Drake was mesmerized by her beauty.

"Okay! Well now. Pick up your chin and wipe your mouth. The lady just got here," Tristan said.

"Oh. I'm sorry. That's not very leader-like I guess." Drake's face started to glow red.

"I am flattered." Whisper's wings tucked under one another as she smiled. It would seem that she also found Drake to be quite good looking.

All of a sudden, in came Manjynx and Spex, followed by Tsunami and Froggle, who was sitting upon Tsunami's shoulder. Whisper looked at them come in the huge doors one by one. "And I thought that I was going to be the tallest one here."

Standing at about six foot, eleven inches, Whisper was very tall indeed, but Tsunami towered at eight and a half feet tall. At least she wouldn't feel out of place so much.

"Hello, I am the Water Guardian, Tsunami. You must obviously be Whisper. It's nice to meet you."

"Thank you," she said as she stared. "I am glad you are on our side. I have never met a creature or being quite so large and as massive as you before. Please forgive me if I stare."

"Oh. No worries. I kind of like having a beautiful women checking me out."

"Hey now! Cool your water-self down," Drake said.

"What, like you have a chance," said Tsunami.

"Anyway," Serrat rolled his eyes, "come on, sis, let us go look around."

"Just a moment, Serrat." She gave him a sign with her hand to wait. "Well, gentlemen. Thank you for making me blush and feel welcome. I will be looking around with my brother, until I am needed."

Just then, Serrat fell back into a trance. "Serrat. What is the matter?" Whisper asked as she helped her brother to his feet. "Serrat, are you all right?"

"Yes," he replied with a tired voice. "I had a vision. A war is starting."

"I still do not see how you can be Oracle yet. You have to be sixteen, she told me," she said with a puzzled look upon her face.

"Whisper, I am sixteen now. My birthday was yesterday."

"How, when we just talked about it coming up in two days? It was just this morning." Now she was really confused.

"No, Whisper. You were in that canyon for three days. We started to worry about you."

"Three days? But how? Are you messing with me? You know, because I am the Wind Guardian and I might have to..."

"No! I am being serious. Now please listen to me. I have seen the death of many. I have also seen the death of a prince. Who, I could not tell, but many will mourn over his death. A war over good and evil has begun."

"All right, I will tell the others. Oh, and Serrat? I love you. We will talk later. Stay here and do not leave."

"Okay. Fight well and fly strong. Oh yeah...be safe out there."

"Thank you. I will."

Tsunami poked his head around the corner. "Come on, Whisper. The Twins seem to have found our new spaceships."

"Ships! How cool is that? By the way, who are the Twins," she asked as they made their way to the others.

"They are the Heart Guardians, Shaw and Shayla. They are both mages and pretty powerful too. At least that is what I have been told."

They went around the corner of a hallway near the portal room. When they reached the chamber room entrance, they both stared in awe. There were five ships specially designed for each Elemental Guardian. Each one matched the armor of the Guardian it was designed for. Shaw and Shayla were sitting in their ship, getting familiar with it, when Drake asked them to come out and gather around the control center. As they got out, they saw Tsunami and Whisper in the doorway. They made their way to the others.

"Hi. My name is Shaw and that is my sister, Shayla," he said as he floated at eye level with Whisper.

"Hello. Nice to meet you. My name is Whisper. You are quite handsome, young warrior. And you are very beautiful, Miss Shayla."

Shayla's face turned red. "Thank you. You are very beautiful as well. I like your name too."

"Yes! Now that we have all met each other, we have some work to do," Drake said. "Shaw and Shayla, I need you to stay here and watch over Serrat."

"Serrat," Whisper interrupted. "He mentioned a war party of ships was coming and he mentioned that a prince was going to die. We must act fast."

"Tristan and Tsunami...you two stay behind Whisper and me, just until we reach Mortox. Then we will break off into separate groups accompanied by the Goyan sky fleets. Is everyone in agreement?"

"Yes, sir," they all answered at once.

"Let's do this then. It's time to show our enemies the true meaning of Elemental Power."

As everyone got into their ships, Whisper kneeled down to Shayla. "Please take care of my brother. He is not a fighter. Let me know if there are any problems."

"I will. I promise to keep him safe."

"Thank you."

"Whisper, we must get going," said Tristan.

"I am coming." Then she smiled at Shayla and climbed into her ship. As she put her helmet on and locked in, she could hear Drake speaking.

"It looks like we place our Crystals of guidance into the front panel."

One by one, they placed their Crystals where they went. Then, one by one, they all powered up. Not only did they power up, but it was as though the ship also became a part of them. Whatever they thought, the ship performed the action. They could use their thoughts to fly the ships. As they all became familiar with their ships, two doors located above them opened up.

"Is everyone ready to go and do this?" asked Drake.

"Ready," said Tristan.

"Ready," Whisper also said.

Let's get these toys goin'. It is time to show everyone the true power of the Zenular Lights," Tsunami said as he lifted his ship off the ground first.

It looked as though it was floating on water. Then Tristan lifted his ship off the ground. It looked as though it was atop a sandstorm. Finally, Drake and Whisper both came off the ground together. Drake's ship had fire and heat under his ship, while Whisper's began to fade in and out like the wind. As they all exited the bay doors from above, the Twins stood there and watched in amazement.

## Chapter 5
## The Guardians Prevail

The battle had been going on for a while now. The Guardians had been fighting together to protect Mortox from the enemy attacks on Goyan. While they were busy trying to protect Prince Lathius from being killed, word came over the radio that Prince Chezeron of the Clave Kingdom was killed in battle. This news brought sorrow across many different lands within the planetary system. He was well known for his crusades to stop the forces of space pirating all around. He helped save many lives and treasures that pirates had taken. If only Serrat's vision had been more clear, but what can you do? There are times that people can be helped, but at the same time, there are those whom you cannot help. Sometimes you will also come across those who do not want to be helped. This was one that the Guardians could not have helped. This is all part of life and sometimes we must deal with the things life gives us. Just keep in mind, life will still go on.

"Drake, did you hear that?" Tristan asked over the radio.

"Yes. Copy that, Tristan. After this battle is over, we shall pay our respects to his family. How is everyone? Tsunami, what is your status?"

"I'm doing just fine, my friend. The Goyan fighters and I have things under control here."

"Copy that. How about you, Whisper? What is your status?"

"We had a couple of close calls, but these Goyan fighters have been exceptional so far. Their tactical maneuvers are better than I imagined. How about you? Are you doing all right?"

"I will let you know in just a moment," he said as fighters surrounded Drake's ship. Just as he was about to send out a shockwave of fire, a meteor shower took out the ships on both sides of him. "Where did…" Then, before he could finish his sentence, Tristan passed over the top of him.

"I thought you could use some help. Looks like I was right." He laughed as he turned his ship around to come back towards Drake.

"Yeah! Thanks. You showed up right in time." Drake fired his rear canons. They sent out balls of fire, which took the shape of several small phoenixes. As they hit the enemy's ships, they cut right through them like butter.

"That was quite some good shooting there, Drake," Tristan said as he was in pursuit of the remaining two ships. This time when he fired, the shots came out like spikes, headed right towards the enemy's engines. As they hit each one, the engines exploded, causing the ships to explode as well.

"Thank you for helping me take out trash. Let's go see if we can help elsewhere."

"Yes, sir. I will follow you."

As they began to head out, a call came over the radio. It was Shayla.

"Hey, guys. I think you should come back to the palace. I found something in the portal room that you need to take look at."

"What is it, Shayla? We are kind of busy right now," Tsunami answered. He and Whisper were working together with their powers. As Tsunami shot a blast of water bombs towards a big star fighter, Whisper used her power of wind to send these now frozen ice bombs sailing at high speeds. As they hit the ship at high velocity, they ripped right through it. The ship began to break apart, destroying it.

"Well, come as soon as you have the chance then," Shayla said.

"Okay, Shayla. We are on our way. I think the Goyan fighters have it from here," Whisper answered. "Let's go back to the base, Tsunami."

"After you, my lady."

"Why thank you."

"Do not mention it."

Then Drake got back on the radio. "We are clear to go here. Tristan and I are heading back too."

\* \* \*

As they headed back to the base, Valladamier and six bounty hunters were on their way to Mortox, where he had his own plans. Whatever he had in mind, the Guardians had better find out soon, because whatever Valladamier was planning would happen soon enough. For he was not too far from Mortox. Maybe thirty minutes or so.

\* \* \*

Back at the palace, the Guardians landed one by one within minutes. Shayla and Shaw were both waiting in the launch bay. There was a door opened, revealing an entrance to the portal room. This was where the Twins were standing.

"When did you find this door?" Tristan asked.

"Serrat found it with his keen eyesight," answered Shaw. "He fell against a lever in the portal room."

"He fell? How? Is he all right?" Whisper asked in concern for her little brother.

"Oh yes. He was playing with Spex. They were playing hide-and-seek."

"Spex was playing hide-and-seek again? I swear that he loves that," said Tristan.

"Yeah, well, he is really good at hiding. Besides, we all like trying to find him," said Shayla. "That is not why I asked you back here though. I found some ancient writing on the Guardians' table. It was covered by a lot of dust, like everything else around here. Follow me and I'll show you." Everyone started towards the table. "I found it while I was cleaning."

"Wow, this place looks really great. Who helped you?" asked Tsunami, smiling at Shayla.

"No one, but I did use a little magic though."

"So what does it say?" Drake asked.

"From what I can tell, it says that if we all place our Crystals of guidance into the proper places at once, it will activate a sort of shield of light around our kingdom. I am not quite sure how far it will reach outside, but it requires all of our Crystals at once."

"Let's all put our Crystals in their places then and see what happens," Drake said. Then they all took their Crystals and put them down upon the table at the same time. The Crystals began to glow until, one by one, a beam of light shot out of them and straight up into the sky. Red, blue, green, white, and champagne pink lit the sky above. The beam surrounded the Mortox Moon and all of the Craixe planet, as it created a force field around them.

Then an urgent call came over the radio. It was a call from Emperor Miethius himself. "Guardians, I see that you have created a shield around our moon and planet, but I am afraid it is too late. For my evil cousin, Valladamier, and his bounty hunters have somehow managed to kidnap my son. I need your help to get him back. Before it is too late for him." Miethius was panicked.

"We are on our way. Stay put until we get there," Drake said.

As they headed for their ships, Whisper saw Serrat sitting in a corner, holding a helmet of a Guardian. He had a look of terror upon his face.

"Serrat. What is wrong?" asked Whisper. He did not answer. "Talk to me, my brother. What ails you?"

Then he came closer and whispered into her ear. She stepped back and shook her head in disbelief, but that is another story.

End of Book 1

# THE FISH OF A THOUSAND CASTS

motor home and sped out of the parking lot leaving only a huge cloud of dust. Smiley paced and stared at the clock like a death row inmate. The Buckmaster violated every known speed law and had the motor home shaking as it threatened to disintegrate at such high speeds.

The clock inched ever closer toward 3:00pm... half an hour to go. Smiley was in full-blown panic mode and asked how close we were every five minutes or so. The Buckmaster knew some back roads that would save time and, to his credit, they did.

At 3:15pm we hit the city limits of Hillsdale. Smiley did his best to get himself cleaned up but it was to little success. There's only so much that you can do with a tomato face and no eyebrows.

Meanwhile at the bride's house, the guests were assembled in the back yard. The bride, it was reported later, was pacing like a caged animal... threatening bodily harm to all seven of us. At 3:25pm she ordered the organ player to start the music.

"I'm going to walk down this aisle whether he's here or not!" she fumed.

My mother and father were in attendance.

"I told you they wouldn't make it!" The Chief said to my mother who bit her lip and nodded in agreement. The wedding march began...

Reverend Jones stood up at the altar as the bride and her father commenced down it. The bride had just reached the altar when the motor home came busting into the driveway.

"Hold on!" shouted The Buckmaster. The motor home screeched into the backyard, tore through a line of bushes and finally ground to a halt just a few feet from the altar. The guests were dumb founded.

The door of the motor home swung open and a number of empty beer cans were deposited onto the lawn. Smiley burst forth from the opening wearing his best flannel shirt.

The rest of us crawled out among the snack wrappers and beer cans and took our seats in the viewing area. The ceremony began and Smiley (tomato faced, eyebrow less and swollen handed) stood there proudly and gazed into his fiancé's eyes. I really don't know if he heard a word of the ceremony . . . he was lost in the moment.

As they said, "I do" I felt a swelling of emotions inside my heart. It wasn't sadness or remorse that I was losing a fellow sportsman, no . . . *I felt happy for him.* Things were changing in the lives of my companions and I; for Smiley and I it was a change for the better! I felt a single warm tear trickle down my face. I warmly remembered my wedding day and recalled that it was the proudest, happiest day of my life. I just wished I would've used my head and married the RIGHT person. I knew what Smiley was feeling and I missed it . . . the feeling, that is, *not* my ex-wife! Heck, after meeting Steph, a wonderful woman who enjoys the outdoors as much as I do, I realize now that marriage isn't *that* bad. Smiley met the right person and it's a beautiful thing!

Another tear trickled down my face and I realized that I was *envious* . . .

*The adventures will continue . . .
God help us!*

Printed in the United States
1130500001B